PENGUIN BOOKS

THE UNMARRIAGEABLE MAN

Ashok Ferrey is the author of five books, all of them nominated for either Sri Lanka's Gratiaen Prize or its State Literary Award. His last book, *The Ceaseless Chatter of Demons*, was longlisted for the DSC Prize for South Asian Literature. By day, he is a personal trainer.

PRAISE FOR *THE UNMARRIAGEABLE MAN*

'Moving easily between Colombo and Brixton in 1980, this fabulous chronicle of Sri Lankan youth sparkles with Ferrey's characteristic lightness of tone, which smuggles in huge emotional impact'—Sir David Hare, playwright

'A joyful ode to a father–son relationship with a cast of colourful characters that dance on the pages, providing a gripping narrative from Colombo to Clapham. Ashok Ferrey serves up a cocktail of secrets and lies, as spicy as coconut sambal'—Shrabani Basu, author of *Victoria and Abdul*

'His prose is so fluid, it takes you along page by page without you ever wanting the story to stop'—Nicole Farhi, designer and sculptor

PRAISE FOR THE AUTHOR

'A wonderful writer'—Alexander McCall Smith, author of the No. 1 Ladies' Detective Agency series

'Laugh-out-loud funny, but also thoughtful, moving and beautifully written. It taught me a lot about Sri Lanka and Sri Lankans'—Ian Rankin (on *Serendipity*), author of *In a House of Lies*

'I particularly enjoyed Ashok Ferrey's witty, punning style'—Michelle de Kretser, author of *Questions of Travel*

'Cosmopolitan and diasporic—at home in other lands as much as his own'—Shyam Selvadurai, author of *Funny Boy*

'Ashok Ferrey is both the court jester and crown prince of modern Sri Lankan writing . . . infectiously hilarious, seamlessly layered and undeniably Sri Lankan'—Shehan Karunatilaka, author of *Chinaman*

the unmarriageable man

Ashok Ferrey

PENGUIN BOOKS

An imprint of Penguin Random House

PENGUIN BOOKS

USA | Canada | UK | Ireland | Australia
New Zealand | India | South Africa | China

Penguin Books is part of the Penguin Random House group of companies whose addresses can be found at global.penguinrandomhouse.com

Published by Penguin Random House India Pvt. Ltd
4th Floor, Capital Tower 1, MG Road,
Gurugram 122 002, Haryana, India

First published in Penguin Books by Penguin Random House India 2021

10 9 8 7 6 5 4 3 2

ISBN 9780143452324

Typeset in Sabon by Manipal Technologies Limited, Manipal

Printed at Repro India Limited

www.penguin.co.in

To the memory of Tilly Mudalnayake (1926–2019)

PART I

1

'O death, where is thy sting?' asked Phyllis of no one in particular.

They were exhausted after the funeral, all these women who while he lived had circled around him like planets around the sun. He had called them his Satellites of Love. They took this death thing firmly in hand. They chose the coffin—'Not too flashy, dear, but not too cheap either'—boldly countermanding his order of a plain unvarnished box of mango wood planks. They chose the hymns ('Make Me a Channel of Your Peace'), they ordered the flowers. One of them, Myrna, even cooked the mala batha, the traditional funeral dinner of curried dry fish, yellow pumpkin and hot coconut sambal. I could not help but wonder what life would have been like had he married *her*. Richer, definitely; fatter for sure. I had seen her sizing him up towards the end, when his bones were sticking out through his shirt at awkward angles, like a sort of half-finished Dad that I, his son, had put together at a craftwork session one rainy afternoon. For his part, he seemed sublimely unaware of the absurd figure he cut. That was the thing about him: he had always been unaware, supremely disdainful of people for whom these things mattered. No, I could not see him married to her. Nor to any of the others for that matter. He was so essentially of that species common to us at the time in that hot steamy part of the world: the unmarriageable man.

So how did I end up then, being his son? Ah, it is a long story. If you will just bear with me these next few hundred pages I will tell you.

They were not young when they met, my parents, both of them in their early forties. Domenica Gaisford, as my mother was known then, was an Englishwoman who met him while visiting a friend in Colombo. It was a long visit—three months at least—and I could not help but wonder, had she come out here in search of a husband? That was how it was done then, you see. Colombo was a sort of entrepôt of human flesh: the singles bar of the British Empire, the Las Vegas of the Colonies. You met at the Galle Face Hotel, you watched the sunset from the verandah—pink gin in hand—before you crossed the road to St Andrew's Scots Kirk to sign up, all in the space of a week perhaps. They had a much more constructivist and workmanlike attitude to marriage those days, a professional knowledge of the nuts and bolts of the contraption. Of course you were in it for the pleasure of the ride like everyone else, but you were well aware of the mechanics purring underneath. And if love happened to seep in through cracks in the machinery it was a delightful bonus, unexpected but welcome, the sweet grease that made the machine run more smoothly.

In the case of my parents, however, there was this one startling and totally inexplicable difference. She was white and he was black: an extreme act of courage I could not imagine either of them being capable of back in the Sri Lanka of the '50s. But then I did not know them well enough, they were only my parents after all. It is one of the tragedies of my life that I was neither old enough nor mature enough to ask my mother about this before she died. I would have been more sure of getting at least a semblance of the truth out of her.

With him, alas, there was no chance. 'The Colombo Swimming Club only allowed natives through its doors in 1971,' he used to say. 'Barely nine years ago. That is why I don't step in even today. My friend Bevan, who performed his tap dancing act, wasn't allowed to use the shower afterwards.'

My father wrinkled his nose. 'He had to go home smelly.'

'Natives?' I asked. '*Natives*?'

'That's what they called us then, Sanjay. Don't be fool enough to imagine even for a moment that they think of us any differently today.'

'So of course you went and married one of them.'

'Ah,' he said with a theatrical sigh. 'Sleeping with the enemy.' His eyes twinkled, arch with the knowledge of all he knew, all I need never know. 'You needn't worry your pretty little head about that. What matters is the now, the present.' He thumped the kitchen table. 'Never forget that, Sanjay. The present, the present, the present.'

*

But I did worry about these double standards. How could he hold such contrary views, even if he were not much different in this from so many Sri Lankans of his generation? The generation that affected to despise the very people whose manners they emulated, whose accents they adopted, who looked down with supreme disdain upon their fellow countrymen when they failed to live up to those exacting and for the most part imaginary standards?

Of Phyllis he once said, 'You know, Sanjay, I could never dream of marrying anyone who had the sort of accent that rhymed "not" with "note" and "dot" with "dote"?' He shivered slightly.

'Lucky escape,' I agreed. 'For *her*.'

That evening after the mala batha, the Satellites of Love—Myrna, Rani, Phyllis and Kamala—sat around the kitchen table reminiscing, unwilling to leave, even though the dearly departed chief guest had long gone up in smoke. They had fought tooth and nail for his attention while he was alive. It was as if they knew that with him gone they only had each other, that the common enemy was now the world outside their tight circle. It was touching to see them all there, each laying their timid claim, like a wreath of poppies, upon the larger-than-life monument of my father's existence.

'Of course he was *always* a little in love with *me*,' said Phyllis, 'that was the trouble.' She coiled and uncoiled her hair—still luxurious after all this time—but her face showed the wear and tear of unkind years, the face of a princess who might indeed have lain asleep a hundred years, though not in the restorative ambience of a fairy tale. My father had called her his Sleeping Beauty. He had not meant it kindly.

As for me, I sat there in silence, with one sentence going round and round in my head like the reverberations of a drum in an empty room. *What do I do now? What do I do now? What do I do now?*

Finally I could take it no longer. 'Ladies,' I said getting up. 'I don't know about you, but I'm off to bed. I'm knackered. Will the last one turn off the lights and shut the front door?'

'Come here, Big Feller,' they said. I went around, kissing each of them in turn. Rosewater and Chanel No. 5, Oil of Ulay and 4711 Eau de Cologne—the collective scent of the mother I had never been lucky enough to have.

*

The funeral festivities went on and on: the seventh day *dhana*, the memorial mass, the endless visits by random strangers claiming to have known him from another life. Since I could not recall having met any of them before, their stories rang hollow. They could probably see the disbelief in my face but that did not stop them. My father was the man of the moment and everyone wanted their piece of him. They wanted to boast loudly of how they had known him the way no one else had. I didn't mind the Satellites, they were family. But this was something else. In Sri Lanka, nothing succeeds like death—it is the ultimate validation. The man you hate in life becomes instantly your idol in death. Any neglected artist can take heart; reviled whilst alive, he only has to wait patiently for death to become the national hero he has always yearned to be.

But where did this leave me? I was exhausted. Exhausted by these fictive accounts of my father's devilry, his bravery, his generosity. Exhausted by the theft of what should have been my sole possession, my narrative.

'Stop! Enough!' I wanted to shout. 'My father was none of these things. You didn't know him the way I did. For the most part, he was a mean old bastard even though I loved him dearly.'

There is an unwritten law in this country that a funeral guest cannot be turned away. These professional mourners—and there were many—began settling into odd corners of the house. They were eating me out of house and home. The kitchen cupboards were bare. The home-cooked food the Satellites brought every day to feed me was being consumed by perfect strangers, with admirable grief and gusto. It was tricky going into the kitchen. You could be trapped in there for hours by bogus individuals with their highly polished tales, tall and colourful.

The Satellites began to complain about their stolen thunder. Most of all, I could hear my father's voice in my head: 'Shyster, conman! Get out of my house. Tell them, Sanjay. Tell them to go this very instant!'

Of course I couldn't (how I longed for my father then!). I was the weak son, as he had always been at pains to point out, so how could I? All I knew was that drastic action was needed. And the solution, when it was finally put to me, was so simple that I wondered why I had not thought of it before.

2

If you close your eyes and try to imagine the ugliest building you can think of, you will most probably picture the British High Commission on Galle Road: a glass box with concrete fins, bold and brash, conceding nothing to the aesthetic of our rather beautiful local architecture. I have come an hour early, expecting to be first in the queue. In fact the queue stretches all the way down the pavement to the Methodist Church at Colpetty Junction. It is now eight in the morning and we are being boiled, fried and grilled in equal measure under the tropic sun. There are people who have been here since five. An easy atmosphere of camaraderie, ruefulness and rumour sweeps up and down the line like a Mexican wave: we're all in this together, we think; it is Us against Them. A black Morris Minor taxi draws up to the kerb and a woman from the queue rushes into it. I see inside a scuffle of arms and legs. Who is she fighting? Is it worth it? She emerges minutes later, triumphant and glamorous though slightly dishevelled, having changed from the kaftan and rubber slippers she was wearing at dawn into more suitable attire. Visa-seeking attire.

This wave of positive energy is there to counteract the tragic loss of face every Sri Lankan feels when we are made to stand on a public pavement under the hot sun, in full view of passers-by. *Why should we feel this?* I do not know, but we do. It is a loss of dignity, a shaming that must stem from our feudal mindset. It is like being put into the stocks on the village green and exposed to public ridicule. In more modern parlance, it is like being caught with one's trousers down in front of strangers, or being heard farting at the dinner table. What this trial by fire and shame means—and perhaps this is what the Brits have meant it to mean—is that obtaining a UK visa is more prized than attaining nirvana. Though possibly a whole lot more expensive.

'Your mother was UK-born?' The visa officer rifles through the contents of my limp brown cardboard file.

'She was English actually. White English.'

He winces. You can use the word 'black' and be proud of it—*I am black, my father is black*—but you cannot use the word 'white' in the same way because it has the taint of supremacy to it. I am beginning to realize that I have a lot to learn.

'And you have never been to the UK?'

I shake my head.

'You are entitled to it. By descent.' He looks at me in disbelief. To be offered nirvana on a plate and spurn it!

'It was never on our radar,' I explain. 'It was too expensive. My father always said I would never get the visa.'

'He told you wrong.'

Bastard, I say under my breath.

'What's that?'

'Nothing.'

'I will issue you a Certificate of Patriality, with the Right of Abode. Once you go there you can apply for full citizenship.'

After my A-levels I had tentatively broached the subject of going abroad to university.

'They'll never let you in, Sanjay,' my father had said. He extended his brown hand so it ran alongside mine. 'You're a *native*, just like me.'

Why? I keep asking myself as I walk back home along Galle Road. I don't care at this point how many old uncles see me shamefully exposed on a public road and toot their horns. Why would he do this to me? Had he wanted me as a sort of house slave, to look after him in his old age? Could he not bear the thought of my defecting, even in some small measure, to the English side? *Why? Why?* I feel a surge of murderous anger. I want to tie him to a chair, turn on the floodlights and grill him. The truth has always been in short supply in our household. Now, with my father gone, there is no chance whatsoever of recovering even a suspicion of it.

*

Myrna had arranged for me to stay with her son in London till I found my own place. The night before I left she turned up with a holdall, out of which she unpacked with great care a number of jars and bottles: seeni sambal, Maldive fish sambal, curry powder and two tall bottles of Passiona cordial. Finally, there was a parcel of fried fish scrunched up in tin foil.

'For when you get hungry on the plane,' she explained.

'They'll feed me on the plane,' I said. 'And you know I'm going through Italy?'

'Italy? You'll definitely need the fried fish then.' Like all good Sri Lankans she had no great faith in other people's cuisines.

'Funny,' I mused, 'all these years and I never knew you had a son.'

She straightened up then, her chin in the air, and looked at me through half-closed eyes. 'Your father wasn't the only man in my life,' she said with quiet dignity.

*

As I kicked my holdall along in the immigration queue at Heathrow, cursing Myrna for overloading me like a donkey, I looked at my passport. It smelt like a freshly minted banknote. There was the Italian visa, and just one other sticker on it: white with a swirly blue line at the top and bottom. 'Certificate of Entitlement to the Right of Abode', it said, above a crown watermark. It was signed G. Fawcett.

The officer inserted a fingernail underneath it, gently attempting to prise it off. 'How did you get this?'

I shrugged. 'The High Commission in Colombo. My mother was English. She was w . . . born in England.'

'Where is she now?'

'She died when I was young.'

'I'm sorry to hear that. So what're you going to do here? Where will you live?'

'In a place called Clapham. With a friend. Hopefully he'll help me find a job.' I didn't want to point out that if I had the unqualified right to live here, the officer didn't have the right to ask me anything else. But I knew enough not to argue with Immigration. She handed back the passport and waved me through, rather grandly.

*

I got down at Clapham North tube station and made my way up Bedford Road, past the Baptist Church and under the railway bridge, with my cardboard suitcase and clinking-clanking holdall, like a sort of immigrant male bag lady. I had seven thousand pounds worth of travellers' cheques in the inside pocket of my shiny anorak (I had found that he wasn't so badly off after all, the mean old skinflint, when I went to clear his bank account). I had never felt so light and free in my life.

Behind Myrna's back the other Satellites had warned me: 'You're going to one of the worst areas of London, Big Feller. Are you sure this is what you want?' But looking at the stately old houses of soft stock brickwork and sandstone trim, with their quiet air of distinction, I found this hard to believe. Later on I was to learn that those grand unblemished facades were only wearing a sort of bricks-and-mortar make-up, one that concealed all the sins of the world: housing the unemployed and the unemployable, some of whom would end up being thrown out of those very windows by rapacious landlords for non-payment of rent.

The house I arrived at was perhaps the most beautiful on the road, its gold stone carving soft and crisp as frozen butter, laid like a garnish across the pale yellow brickwork. The man who opened the door to me was balding with frizzy hair, an incongruously fluffy pink towel draped around his midriff. He looked at least as old as Myrna.

'Janak?' I asked with a smile.

He shook his head. 'Janak was running late for his shift. I'm Deva. He asked me to let you in.'

The air inside was humid and frowsty with the animal smell of bodies. He led me past the long ground-floor room that ran from front to back. In the gloom I could make out a row of mattresses on the floor, laid side by side all the way to the rear window. On these, men were lying in their underpants, fast asleep.

'Shift work,' Deva explained matter-of-factly. 'You take whichever mattress is free when you come home.' He must have seen the look of horror on my face because he added quickly, 'Janak has his own room upstairs, right at the top. He's given you his bed.'

'So where will he sleep?'

Deva gestured towards the mattresses. He smiled apologetically. 'This is how it is. Don't worry. We're used to it.'

I clinked and clanked my way up the narrow staircase to Janak's bedroom in the attic. I was only beginning to get an inkling of what lay in store for me, deep in the heart of this wild, wild West I found myself in.

3

You see Colombo now—cranes and half-built towers everywhere and Chinese workers in yellow hats walking their familiar duckwalk—and you have no idea how it was for us in those early days. I cast my mind back and see the skies of that older town tinctured in the colours of violet and old rose. I see the soft thick green of its hedges, that twilight green of fairy-tale forests. If there are parapet walls, they are only three feet high; and on either side of every road giant trees, leaning drunkenly towards each other, gossiping. So that walking beneath, you are in the narrow high nave of some forest cathedral. I hear the harsh cries of hot-weather birds and the tuneless whistle of bats swooping home to roost in the park. It is a much more cosmopolitan town than now—white, red, yellow, black—with English very much its lingua franca. A town where people cycle or walk (at what point did it come to signify such a loss of face to be seen walking?) and the occasional fat lady with shopping parcels smiles benignly upon you while being pulled along in a rickshaw by a stringy brown man. Of course you will say I am seeing it all through rose-tinted glasses, but when was the past ever not? I remember this too: a cyclist sweeping past a woman near our house, snatching the gold chain off her neck in one graceful movement; so perhaps it wasn't such a safe town either.

My father and I lived in a painfully modest house on Clifford Road, Colpetty, built with my mother's money in the '50s, when they got married—the brutal utilitarian '50s when concrete was king and ornament its enemy. He was extremely proud of his Burma teak flush doors and his reeded glass windows. To me it was solid and unpretentious and dull, missing all the eccentric loveliness of those older colonial bungalows, of which there were so many back then. Indeed, if you had heard my father speak—the flamboyance of his speech, the acidity of his wit—you would be hard-pushed to imagine him living in such a house. Perhaps it had the stamp of my mother all over it? Who knows? She was gone long before I could tell.

But I remember how the house stood then: its polished red-oxide floors, its Bengal carpets, its mid-century modern chairs each upholstered a different colour in some knobbly faux-leather material; and at the far end a single black wall on which hung a circular white iron-framed mirror. After my mother's death my father simply stopped caring for the house, and we who lived in it failed to see its decline. You might have thought the Satellites would be goaded into action with mops and pails and Vim, but the shabbiness of the house, its picturesque squalor and decay, must have been an essential part of the dream they were hoping to buy into. Or perhaps they were wise enough to know that you can't teach an old dog new tricks. And my father was a very old dog by then. Or so he seemed to me.

Money was always in short supply. My father was a naturally stingy man and he used this scarcity as a sort of shrine to his tight-fistedness. It never seemed to have occurred to him that he could go out and get himself a decent job. Whenever I wanted anything extra, he would open his eyes wide—the eyes of the all-knowing ingénue, the image he liked to present to the outside world—and ask, 'So, where do you think the money's going to come from? Heaven?'

But young as I was, I could see he took a certain pleasure in depriving me of those little luxuries—the tube of Smarties, the pack of multicoloured glass marbles—that might have meant so much to a child. As for himself he was a man of simple means, able to get by on very little, so the deprivation didn't mean much to him.

My father relied for his income on the rental of two small cottages in Moratuwa, a distant suburb of Colombo from where his family had originally come. There was never a time when he wasn't squabbling with those poor benighted creatures his tenants. His life was one long litany of leaking roofs and unpaid rents. He collected his dues promptly on the first day of each month but spent much of the preceding month in anticipation of rents denied, polishing up the invective he would hurl at them in this rather likely event. At times it got very personal.

'Never trust a vegetarian,' he would shout, shaking his fist at the shaving mirror. Or, 'What do you expect of a man who chews betel! Betel, ha! Have you seen his mouth? It's all red and rotted!'

He would return from these collection trips like an explorer out of Africa, exhausted but flushed with success, his eyes feverish with the exertion, brandishing two cheques (or not, as the case may be). I swear if he had ever got himself decent tenants who paid on time, happy to live uncomplaining within those termite-ridden walls, my father would have died of shock. He chose his tenants with great care, assessing them closely for their potential quarrelsomeness, and in the main he succeeded.

*

I woke up to the powdery winter light cast by the attic window directly overhead. There was a man standing over me, frozen in a dramatic pose, brandishing a bottle of Passiona.

'Janak?' I asked. 'Sorry, I must have dropped off with the jet lag.'

'Sanjay?' he whispered. 'You must be Sanjay.'

'Why are we whispering?' I whispered.

'Because we don't want to wake you up,' he whispered and smiled. And when he smiled, a gentle sweet smile, he looked exactly like his mother.

'Myrna sends you her love. You've been promising to visit these last three years. Please come, she says.'

'And she's been promising to visit *me* these last three years,' he smiled again. 'You can tell her that when you return. Anyway I must get back to the kitchen. Dinner in an hour. And I'll take these down if I may.' Hugging the holdall to his chest he disappeared in a great rumble of bottles.

I discovered there was another room on the ground floor in the small back addition to the house, extended—by a Sri Lankan handyman, no doubt—with two improvized corrugated iron sheets. Janak was stirring up an enormous pot of curried goat. Random shift workers turned up, each of them treated to a ladleful of indeterminate goat pieces heaped upon a mound of basmati. Everyone ate with their fingers, standing up, and no one took longer than five minutes to eat. There was no such thing as dinner-time conversation. I could almost hear my father turning in his grave. Having nothing better to do I hung around watching all this.

In the few days that I stayed there, I don't think I spoke more than half a dozen words to any inhabitant. It was hard to identify them for a start: they came and went, replacing each other on any available mattress. It didn't seem to interest them that I was a fellow countryman. Perhaps their lives were so hard, their struggles so uphill, they didn't have the luxury of introducing any extraneous knowledge into their closely circumscribed existences.

'Where do they work?' I asked Janak.

He shrugged. 'At petrol stations all over south London. Cash in hand, no questions asked. I can fix you up too if you like?'

I shook my head. 'Give me a week. I'll take you up on your offer if nothing better comes along.'

Many of my father's friends had emigrated to the UK in the '50s and '60s as a consequence of disastrous Sri Lankan-government policies. They had been mostly doctors, lawyers and engineers. White-collar emigrants. This current blue wave was something new.

'They aren't very friendly, are they?' I said.

Janak looked at me a little sternly. 'You wouldn't be either, if you were working illegally and didn't want to give too much away. But one thing I can tell you. They pay their lodging fees very promptly.' He went on to explain how he was the official tenant of the premises, the others his sub-tenants. The Indian landlord was happy with this arrangement, not having to deal with the illegals himself, so that nominally at least he didn't get his hands dirty. Whatever Janak made over and above (and he hinted that it was a substantial amount) was his to keep.

'Does your mother know?' I asked, shocked.

He threw up his hands in a gesture both futile and magnificent. 'What does anybody in Sri Lanka know about the realities of living in this so-called First World?'

Privately I resolved to get out as soon as I could. I felt sorry for Janak who was caught in this trap. He had, after all, willingly given up his room for me, which was unfair on him. I am ashamed to admit there were other reasons too, things about the house that offended my rather middle-class sensibilities. (Perhaps I was more my father's son than I cared to admit.) In the tropics, we were unused to such things as closed windows, unless there was a tropical deluge. Here in the Brixton of the '80s, there seemed to be no such thing as an open one. Opening a window meant losing heat, that precious commodity which had to be paid for with coins in the slot meter. Everywhere you went inside that house you got the faintly foetid smell of unmade bed mingling with the acrid odours of roasted fenugreek and melted goat fat. Any new smell simply overlaid the old, adding to its depth and complexity. It brought to mind those stock pots I had read about, bubbling away for hundreds of years in the dungeon kitchens of French chateaux. I was not surprised Myrna had not visited.

But I could see that Janak was proud of his little entrepreneurial scheme—even if it hovered uncertainly in that twilight area between landlordism and extortion. Proud too of his somewhat stellar position in this subterranean hierarchy.

'This is the respectable side of Bedford Road,' he said with some satisfaction. 'We're Clapham. That side is Brixton. We don't go there. It's too dangerous.'

*

So naturally next morning I crossed over to the dark side. I walked up Ferndale Road, past Moores the builders' yard, enchanted by the houses on either side: four storeys of the palest pink brickwork, dressed with creamy terracotta; there might have been something Mughal about them, or even Italian, of the Renaissance. Very quickly the pale pink petered out to be replaced by standard yellow stocks, but the impression was of one unending Italian palazzo stretching all the way to infinity, the painted backdrop, perhaps, of some Palladian theatre. Coming from Colombo where houses were idiosyncratic, chaotic and individual, I had never before seen a street that worked so magnificently as one architectural construct. It blew me away. I had never particularly thought about becoming an architect ('Oh, Sanjay, get those damned fool ideas out of your head!' said my father), but I had read everything about the subject I could lay my hands on. I was attracted to it because it seemed to lie, as nothing else did, at that precise mid-point between art and mathematics.

I took a right on to Tintern Street and immediately the houses got smaller. The regularity remained but these houses were only two storeys high, and the unchanged street width gave them a stable air that was almost Grecian in its serenity. There was a small shop at the corner. I pushed open the door, a bell ringing above me.

''Allo 'andsome!' said a rather gruff voice. 'What can I do you for today?'

I smiled politely at the middle-aged Asian woman in a salwar-kameez and flamboyantly hennaed hair, stacking the shelves. 'Just looking, thanks.'

Who needed Myrna's bottles? Everything you wanted was here: Portuguese bacalao and Jamaican callaloo and even ikan bilis from Malaysia.

'By the way,' I asked, 'do you know of anyone around here who'll rent me a room?'

She threw her head back and laughed. 'Knock on any door, love. Anyone'll give you a room. Around here they all need the money. Except me, that is. I'm rich. And me old man would kill me if he saw you. Sri Lankan, innit?'

I was surprised. 'How did you know?'

'Better-looking than us Indians. Fitter!'

Behind the tins of jackfruit I saw a public telephone. I almost said, 'Can you change a fiver, I need to call home?' Then I remembered. There was no one at home now to call.

As I opened the door to leave, she said casually, 'Try old Mr Brown at 23. Say that Bilquis sent you. He'll find room to fit you in, I'm sure.' She chortled with merriment and the glass bangles on her plump arms tinkled in consensual delight.

*

The bell did not seem to be working, so I knocked. Nothing. I rattled the letter box. Then I knocked again. From deep inside I could hear a slow rhythmic wheeze, getting louder, as if someone were slowly pumping up a bicycle tire. On the other side of the frosted glass I could make out a blurry black figure. Then the wheezing stopped. He was listening to me listening to him.

'Go away!' he said through the letter box. 'I have enough of you already. There's too many of you here!'

'Too many?' I exclaimed, stung by this pre-emptive racist strike. (And from a black man in Brixton too.) 'I only want a room,' I shouted back. 'The lady at the shop said you might have a room for me, Mr Brown?'

The wheezing began again. 'Bilquis?' I heard him muttering. 'Room?' He drew the bolts back and opened the door. The chill struck me. It was like walking into a freezer. 'What do you want a room for?'

'Please,' I said desperately. 'I've just arrived in the country. I need somewhere to stay.'

He took off the black felt hat he was wearing and began scratching his head. Very thoroughly. For a long time. Then he turned slowly and walked back in. He had not invited me in, but he hadn't closed the door on me either, so I followed. He stopped at the staircase and leant heavily on the newel post. The wheezing stopped and I held my breath. Then he began to climb, one step at a time—step, wheeze, step. I followed, falling easily into the rhythm. After about a week we reached the first landing. He turned and looked at me.

'I can't manage them stairs,' he said.

'You're telling me.'

He threw open the nearest door and said, 'Your room.'

It was completely bare. No bed, no curtains, not even a lightbulb on the ancient black woven flex dangling sorrowfully from the ceiling.

'It's great!' I said smiling. 'How much do you want, Mr Brown?'

He began scratching his head again. I held on to that bright smile for dear life, not daring to drop it in case he changed his mind. It was painful.

Finally he said, 'Twenty pound. A month.'

'I'll take it,' I said quickly.

I didn't care that there was no bed, gave no thought to how I was going to feed myself in a non-existent kitchen; and it was an extremely good thing I did not check out the bathroom. But I had a room in the big city. I was home.

Little did I know then that I had just laid my hands on the tail of the dragon: one that was to take me twisting and hurtling through those glorious, blue-rinsed Thatcher '80s, breathing fire on everything we looked at, conquering all, scorching all, on what was to be the ride of my life.

'You can have the whole upstairs, man,' Mr Brown said. 'I don't come up here no more. It very quiet.'

He took the first step of his laborious descent down. Then he turned around. 'If they try to make too much noise, you say, "Shoo! Go way!" They frightened of big feller like you. They frightened.'

4

'There's something in my throat. I'm finding it difficult to swallow,' my father announced. He was hunched over his Philips transistor radio amidst the clutter on the dining table, in an attitude of prayer. This was only right because that radio was more precious to him than any son, the BBC World Service satisfying his spiritual needs more fully than any church service. When the 'Lilliburlero' came on—the theme tune—it was like a summons to holy mass.

'Your throat?' I said. 'You old hypo! Always complaining about something or other, aren't you?'

'I've had this for the last couple of days. I haven't breathed a word.'

'How brave. We'd better get you to a doctor then, hadn't we?'

His GP, Dr Nava, lived at the end of the road, a mild-mannered, harassed woman he'd been seeing for the last thirty years at least. They had a formal if strained relationship. In the old days she would drop everything and come to him the moment he called.

Over the years there had been so many false alarms that she now absolutely refused to pay house calls, insisting that he come to her instead.

'But doctor, I'm dying!' he would exclaim.

'Die then. Please. Be my guest,' she would reply.

'Lazy cow,' he would mutter darkly. 'You shouldn't be a doctor if you have such a callous nature.'

At the surgery he would blithely sail in, seemingly unaware of the twenty or so patients who had come before him, waiting grimly outside, some of whom I am sure really were dying.

'There's nothing wrong with you,' the doctor would tell him.

'But doctor, my pressure? You forgot to check my pressure.'

With the resigned air of a Christian martyr Dr Nava would take out the pressure kit, wrapping the canvas around his arm. She pumped it up. 'Quite normal,' she said triumphantly. 'See?'

Only then would my father get up. 'I feel so much better already. Thank you, doctor.' He gave her his dazzling Hollywood smile (he still had very good teeth). 'You have healing hands, you know that? See you very soon, doctor.'

'I sincerely hope not,' she would mutter under her breath.

My father flashed another gracious smile at those in the waiting room as he left. He knew the door between the surgery and waiting room was kept permanently open—so that all could share in the minutiae of his very personal problems: it encouraged bravura performances on his part. It was immensely satisfying to talk about erratic bowel movements to a captive audience.

This time around the doctor said nothing. She poked a small torch down his throat. She pressed gently around his neck. Then on letter-headed notepaper she began to write in silence. Putting the letter into a brown envelope she handed it to me. 'See Dr Karu at St Xavier's,' she said. 'Your father needs to have a biopsy done. There is a growth on the pharynx.'

My father looked at the doctor, then at me. For once he was at a loss for words. Was there a small look of triumph in his eyes? I could imagine what he was thinking: all these years I've been trying to tell you, all these years. You never believed me, you never listened. Now see? But the triumph was drowning in genuine fear.

'It's standard procedure,' I said as we walked home. 'There's nothing wrong. They just have to check.'

'What do you know,' he said quietly.

All my life he had kept me firmly in my place, enjoying the quiet luxury of patronizing me, pitying me. I could feel this changing now—the ground shifting under my feet, the balance of power realigning. For the first time in my life I felt sorry for him: though it was not something I found myself revelling in.

*

It is strange how your world can flip in just one instant from its sparse but essentially well-ordered self: into one of whirling chaos, perfumed by anaesthetic and disinfectant, presided over by brazen nurses in short skirts and severe matrons in long; a world of plastic folders and perpetual motion, of steps echoing down corridors blue-lit and unearthly. You realize you are now on a war footing, that time as you once knew it has ceased to exist. But the really surprising thing is that this world has always existed, invisible to you till now, parallel and simultaneous, there but not there. The world of the dead and the dying. Having once descended it becomes so normal to you that when you do come up eventually, you find it is the real world that is abnormal and unreal; and it takes a long, long while before you are fully decompressed, re-oxygenated.

'The good news,' said Dr Karu, 'is that the growth is round and smooth like a marble, not curly like a cauliflower.'

'Nothing like a good cauliflower,' my father sighed. His eyes were unhealthily bright. Only I knew what an effort he was making.

'We'll take you in for the biopsy tomorrow.'

'What? So soon?' My father sounded like a jovial host prevailing upon a dinner guest to stay a little longer.

'In cases like these, it is inadvisable to wait. We'll schedule it for tomorrow afternoon. It'll be under general, so no food or drink for the next twenty-four hours.'

'And I was so looking forward to my roast beef sandwiches this evening.'

Dr Karu looked at him for a moment, puzzled, not getting the full measure of the man. My father's charm was wasted on him.

Just before the operation, the anaesthetist came out to speak to me as his next of (and only) kin. 'Your father has an enlarged aorta, an arrhythmic heartbeat. I must warn you that he may not come out of the anaesthetic.' She produced a sheaf of papers. 'If the operation is to proceed, you must give your consent.'

I should like to tell you that I was cool and sober, judiciously weighing the pros and cons. The truth, however, is that your heart is firing like a machine gun. You cannot breathe. The patient is on the table, the doctor gowned. Your head is about to burst with the pressure.

I remembered my father saying once, 'We're an odd lot, my boy. We all have enlarged hearts. My father had it, I have it. You probably have it too. Too much love, that's what it is. We all have too much love to give.'

'Go ahead with the operation,' I said, signing the form. 'It's a congenital thing. We'll take the risk.'

Right then, I could have done with a Satellite or two for moral support, but my father had expressly forbidden it. 'I can't have a gaggle of old women around me, Sanjay,' he said. 'Fussing like hens.'

I wondered why. He who had never been above taking advantage of their kindness and generosity—even the roast beef had come from Myrna—was suddenly fighting shy. Then it dawned on me. All this talk of illness had in some way unmanned him. It was a loss of face to have bits of you cut out. I would not have cared in the slightest, but he was a different man altogether. Any admission of a faulty part meant some intrinsic flaw in the whole. His standing with the Satellites would never be the same again (or so he must have felt). The people I needed most by my side were precisely the ones I was not allowed to turn to.

The results were ready a week later. I went to meet Dr Karu. Alone.

'Your father has cancer,' he said shortly. He began writing another letter. Our lives were full then of these mysterious, interminable letters that were not for us to read—for the most part they were illegible—but for us to deliver to other gatekeepers in this subterranean world. They carried the secret codes to our lives, which we were not party to—terms like 'haemoglobin' and 'lymphocyte' and 'full blood count'. They were the visas that on production opened doors to other corridors, other tunnels. The fact that these letters might destroy or refashion our lives was of little concern to those who wrote them, even less to those who read them. Lives were an expendable commodity down here, a minor irritant easily done away with, the oxygen you breathed in only to expel with a whoosh. The zero in the algebraic equation that, quite literally, meant *nothing*.

*

With Janak's help I moved in that weekend. When I say moved in, I mean the one suitcase that I dragged around. That was it. There was a junk shop by the railway arches at Clapham North where Janak found me two beds at a fiver apiece.

'I only need one,' I pointed out.

'They're matching,' he replied. 'And you never know.'

A few doors down was an estate agency, Clapham Estates. The window was plastered with cards. It seemed that everyone in the area was trying to sell and get out. The going rate for a house was anything between twenty and thirty thousand pounds. Next door was a shop selling kitchen appliances, second-hand, some even in fairly good nick. In spite of the wintry weather it was all out there on the pavement, everything you could want for a halfway decent life. I thought to myself: no wonder the illegals liked this area. It was rather like living in a Western version of the Pettah.

Janak stepped in with his sure-fire instincts and snapped up a gas cooker for me. 'You'll need a plumber for this. I have a number at home.'

Since the beds were not being delivered for another hour he treated me to lunch under the arches at Mandy's Caff. 'I come here when I want a curry-free day,' he said. It was eleven o'clock, breakfast hour for the workers, and there was a queue. 'Two mixed fries, please, love,' he told Mandy at the counter.

'Who's this then? New kid on the block?'

Janak winked. 'This one's different. He's regular.'

'Regular? Hah! How disappointing.' She turned to me. 'Try the cherry pie. That'll sort you out.'

On an oval plate was a fried egg, beans, bacon, sausage, tomato, mushrooms, chips and a triangle of fried bread. Cholesterol heaven. I could see that this was a life I could slip into easily, a life so different from the one I had left behind that it felt like being reborn, re-formed. An entirely different language would have to be learnt; I was already able to discern a few rudimentary words of it.

Afterwards, Janak pointed down Clapham Road. 'There's a Sainsbury's at Stockwell. Much cheaper than the corner shops around here.' But I had decided to stick with Bilquis. She was only across the road. And she had found me the room after all.

*

Mr Brown watched our comings and goings from his favourite spot at the newel post, wheezing rhythmically in quiet counterpoint. Upstairs, apart from the one he had shown me, there were two other rooms. The front room overlooking the road was filled with furniture and junk; all of it pretty unusable. In any case it had not formed part of the deal. Next to it was a smaller empty room which I appropriated as my bedroom. I was now the proud proprietor of quite a large flat. For the first time in my life I had a place I could call my own. *Home!* Suddenly, I wanted to be alone in it with

Janak gone: to stretch out and touch every corner of this space, to command its volume, to possess it.

'There's a dance tomorrow,' Janak said before he left, 'the Sri Lanka UK Society. We call them the SLUTS behind their back. Do you want to come?'

When I didn't answer he added, encouragingly as he imagined, 'They're more your sort of people.'

I grinned. 'You mean there'll be no illegals?'

He shrugged. 'Go on. At least they will hold a conversation with you, this lot.'

'Okay,' I said, still unsure.

'My mother will be thrilled that I am introducing you to some *nice* people. She was very particular about that in the last letter.'

After he left I stood silent and still for a whole minute, breathing in the ferocious cold.

5

On those rainy monsoon afternoons, when the Satellites were gathered around my father at the dining table with the Philips droning on at low volume, they would play a little game. *Whom do we marry Sanjay off to?* My father was the principal player, but you needed a quorum of at least two Satellites for a satisfactory session, because between them they had—all stitched up tight—the genealogies and scandals, the sexual predilections and irreversible medical conditions of all Colombo.

The game might begin like this.

'What about Rowena? *Aney*, sweet girl, no? Coconut estate in Kuliyapitiya. Eight plucks a year. Just imagine the money!'

'Are you mad, Phyllis? You want Sanjay's children running around with six toes on each foot? You know the family's famous for that, no? What sort of life would those poor children have?'

'My grandmother—'

'This is not about your grandmother, Phyllis. Everyone knows she led a perfectly blameless life with six toes, but—'

'*But?* What do you mean *but?* What are you trying to insinuate?'

'Girls,' my father would cut in. 'Girls!' He was very good at keeping the peace. So long as he was not the one breaking it.

Things would simmer down for a while. Till someone started up again.

'I hear that Suriya girl is back from London. A first-class in Astrophysics they say.'

'And if you believe that—'

'Mad, of course. Whole family's bonkers.'

'But the father's a Supreme Court judge, surely?'

'Of course. Went to court starkers.'

'You want Sanjay's family to be saddled with insanity?'

'Look who's talking!'

'Take that back. *At once!*'

At this point I would burst out of my room. 'Would you all shut the fuck up? I'm trying to do some reading in here.' I hardly ever used the F-word in front of the Satellites. When I did, it was to devastating effect. I could see Rani's chin wobble. It looked as if she were about to cry. I felt sorry, but it couldn't be helped. As long as they were talking about me I could not help but listen, so it was best they stopped.

I was nineteen years old and did not have a girlfriend. This was not unusual in the Sri Lanka of those days, but that was not the point. I had long ago realized that having a girlfriend and living with my father were two incompatible, mutually exclusive states of being. At the age of sixteen I had once brought a girl home for a study session.

'Who do we have here?' asked my father, brightening up at this unexpected prospect of young female company.

'This is Shamista. We're doing a project together.'

I was about to hustle her into my room when my father blocked our path. 'I hate to point this out, dear, but we must start as we mean to go on, in full possession of facts. Have you noticed his ears?'

'No,' said Shamista. 'What's wrong with his ears?'

'If you hadn't noticed, then that's fine, I won't trouble you any more. Please. Continue with your study.'

There was nothing odd about my ears. They stuck out only a little. But by now they were burning so much that I would have happily cut them off with a kitchen knife.

'Ignore him,' Shamista said.

A few minutes later my father popped his head round the door. His lips were pursed and his face was screwed up with the effort of trying not to laugh.

'Have you had a chance to examine them yet?'

'Get out!' I shouted murderously. He would always find a way to undermine me I realized. It was a sport to him. I was his prey, captive and powerless: it was his house, his money.

So why didn't I move out, you might ask? Couldn't I have got a job—any job, perhaps even as a labourer on a building site—and be on my own?

I am afraid this was not even a remote possibility in the Colombo of the time. Any job I might have landed would not have covered even my lodgings, let alone transport and food. That was how the system worked: you were paid so inadequately that rich or poor, you were expected to live at home in order to survive. That labouring job would have sufficed for half a room in a tenement with no running water or sanitation: things I had got used to in my prison and would not be able to do without. On top of that, strange to say, I had quite grown to love my captor (if indeed you could call it love), learnt how to survive by keeping out of his way without arousing his ire or his whiplash tongue. I was the classic kidnap victim, caught frozen in the headlamps of my captor's sarcasm.

I never brought a girl home again.

This of course provided my father with even more fodder. 'You know how it is with Sanjay,' he would stage whisper to the Satellites with a theatrical wink. 'Late developer. Tread with caution.'

Perhaps he never wanted me to have any relationships of my own. Perhaps my job in life was to be his servant, to look after him in his old age.

To listen to him, his own life was—in dramatic contrast—a shining example of how one ought to live. He had been quite the Romeo in his youth. 'No girl was safe, Sanjay, no girl was safe. Mothers used to lock up their daughters when they knew I was in town!'

I did not believe a word of it. As far as I was concerned, he lived in a world of complete make-believe: a world of dragons and magic potions and damsels in distress, where he was the knight in shining armour, cutting a swathe through this highly coloured historic landscape. The really strange thing was that in public at least, we (the Satellites and I) submitted to this fiction willingly. Even though the private reality was the darkened room with its mildewed walls, its dingy unswept corners, the transistor droning on monotonously, the ceaseless patter of rain outside.

'You know, my boy, I went to school in Sussex?'

'Oh, sure.'

'That is how I learnt to do things properly. The English way. And later on, when I was a young man, Italy. Tuscany . . . all those towns . . . Sansepolcro, San Gimignano, Anghiari. Oh, how I remember Anghiari! I speak Italian, of course. Fluently.'

Lying about at home was a small hardback book, *Teach Yourself Italian*, with a shiny blue and yellow dustcover. I had been obsessed with it for a couple of months, before I got fed up and threw it away. I probably had more Italian than he did.

*

With the cancer, those cozy afternoons simply ceased. The Satellites were mystified. The phone rang and rang in an empty house because my father and I were in hospital all day.

'Where were you?' Myrna asked, square-jawed and indignant. 'I came round with string hoppers and hot mulligatawny. There was no one at home!' A good meal gone waste.

'I'm sorry,' I said guiltily. 'We were out walking on Galle Face Green.'

'What? At eight o'clock at night?'

They were not stupid, these well-meaning women, particularly Myrna. There was not much you could get past her. She watched you patiently, like a dog watching a garden wall at night for polecats. And when she pounced, she pounced with surprising agility. They must have been aware even then of our circumstances. This was only another wayward chapter of the fictional narrative they were being made to subscribe to, while the truth galloped on underneath, following its own unerring course.

*

The next stop was Professor Fernando of ENT Surgery at St Xavier's. I watched his long fingers turning the pages of the report: the fingers of a conductor on the score of a famous symphony. Having conducted it so often he had no real need to look, he knew the score only too well, so to speak. Finally, placing his fingertips together he looked at me with immense concentration. In silence.

After a while I asked anxiously, 'Can you not operate?'

'Operate?' More intense silence. The concerto was playing itself out inside his head.

He said gently, 'Go home. Tell your father to put his affairs in order.'

I waited in case there was more. When I realized there wasn't, I got to my feet. Throughout the entire consultation he had not looked at my father once, speaking to me as if he weren't there. He was already a statistic in a hospital file, I could see that. I bundled him out of there.

But somebody saw us at the hospital and mentioned it to the Satellites because next morning they were all at our door. I could see they had dressed with care, this phalanx of females ready for the joust, ready for the crusade of their lives.

'A second opinion. We need a second opinion,' they declared, tilting at the phrase, knocking it back and forth with gracious feminine chivalry and side-saddle horsemanship. Between them they naturally knew the entire medical fraternity in town. In no time at all they had us 'channelled' to the surgery of Dr Rahman on Norris Canal Road.

'We'll schedule the operation for next Wednesday,' Dr Rahman decided. 'Take this and present it to the General Hospital on Tuesday. They will admit you.' He scribbled on a notepad. Another day, another letter, another hospital.

'By the end of this, you and I will have PhDs in hospital services,' said my father. His joviality rang hollow to me. Perhaps he was convincing enough to the one person that mattered in all of this: himself.

*

You might be tempted to ask me how I write with such levity about these events, the words slipping through my fingers, light and friable, like so many grains of rice in a gunny sack I have plunged my hand into. It's because all this happened many years ago, you tell yourself. He must have got over it by now. After all, doesn't time heal all wounds? He must surely have achieved *closure* by now?

Well, I can answer with the certainty of old age that 'closure' is fiction existing only in the mind of the man who invented it. Let us hope he earned his reward in heaven. Let us hope he achieved his own closure.

There is a whole generation of us today subscribing to the mythic properties of this alchemic substance—distilled in the alembics of modern psychotherapy—that can transform the fool's gold of our sorrow, in a flash of chemical reaction, into something unalloyed and twenty-four-carat. Something at once dead and far-removed; something we can hang on the wall to revere from afar. Where it no longer has the capacity to wound. No longer has the corrosive effects of a grief inconveniently alive.

We are so obsessed with the quick clean end, the end that takes no longer than the length of a Hollywood film, that we have invented this word 'closure' for it—hoping that the truth of this heroic compound will follow shortly after the naming of it. If the word exists, the concept must, mustn't it? But I will tell you differently. All that exists at the end is the sheer animal act of forgetting, and the act of forgiving ourselves for forgetting. It is a physical thing born of years of harrowing repetition and replay: the road so often travelled that the scenery is no longer visible, the paragraph so often read that the sense is no longer apparent.

So, please forgive my flippancy. I only draw the fingernail lightly across the scab. Any harder and I greatly fear the scab will reopen, the virulence pouring out like old black engine oil, poisoning the bloodstream one more time. A risk I cannot afford to take.

*

When I could sleep no longer, lying rigid in bed listening to the snores of the old man in the next room, I discovered running. I would let myself out of the house in the sodium-yellow hours of early morning, up Clifford Road and right on to Green Path, then around the park. Each circuit was a mile and a quarter, and I found I could do five or six of these at a time—I who had never played any sport in my life. I wanted to beat my sorrow into submission, punish it. And in doing so, I wanted to punish myself for my weakness in succumbing to it. After about the fourth round, I found my legs running on their own, this great animal of a body flying in the wind, while the mind floated far above and free, the immense disc of the world rotating slowly beneath of its own accord. The world had nothing to do with me: its sadness, its joys, were not mine; they were unimportant, irrelevant. All there was to me was my mind, dispassionate and disinterested. And sublimely free of sorrow.

6

Janak picked me up at eight. He eyed me critically. 'No suit?'

I shook my head. I had never possessed a suit. My father had been inordinately proud of his suits and shoes, all made in Bristol, or so he claimed—yet one more boast I found difficult to believe. Why Bristol? Because the measurements were apparently sent over on one boat, and the finished products sent back on another. Instead of a jacket I wore my hideously shiny polyester anorak.

We walked through various side roads beyond Tintern Street, and down Acre Lane to the Edwardian splendour of Brixton Town Hall. Negotiating staircases and passages, we ended up in the sort of featureless numberless room that town halls are famous for, haphazardly decorated with bunches of balloons hung here and there, odd arrangements of flowers in corners. It brought to my mind those monthly socials back home at the local parish hall, where I stood awkwardly with my piece of butter cake and plastic cup of Nescafé while my father made delightful small talk with the priest about sin and sodomy.

There was a gaggle of women at the door. 'These are the lovely ladies responsible for this, this delightful decor,' said Janak, deadpan. 'And this is my friend Sanjay.'

'So who's who are you?' they asked, the usual Colombo game before which no conversation with a stranger is permitted. When they found out I was 'Louis' son', they were ecstatic. Each of them brought out of mothballs their Louis story while I shut my ears and composed my face into one of concern and interest. 'No!' I said. 'You're joking! Really? The old devil! How absolutely marvellous!' Perhaps my father's tall tales had not been so tall after all.

'A good man lost,' said one of them with a wink. 'What a waste of a life.'

How dare you be so patronizing! I wanted to say. *Just because you imagine you're living the good life in the imperial capital here? We had our moments, my father and me. It wasn't as bad as you think.* It was okay for me to criticize him; it wasn't okay for others to do the same. But in fact I stayed silent. I had never been a confrontational sort of person. Besides, I had a nasty suspicion that she was referring to something other than the quality of our Colombo life.

To watch them preening themselves, this might have been the London chapter of the Satellites of Love. There was this one difference I noted though. These foreign Satellites were startlingly over-Sri Lankanized:

like '50s starlets with elaborate hairdos involving ringlets and flowers, dressed in saris of yesteryear that nobody back home might wear any more. It struck me then how the home country changes imperceptibly, unbeknownst to the people who have left it, while the émigré retains forever his image of it fixed and static from the time he left. Though their styles might verge on parody there was something terribly touching too, in this sincere effort at recreating the past of their imagination. I thought to myself: exaggeration is the sincerest form of flattery.

Janak hustled me away as soon as he decently could and we found ourselves a table in the corner. 'You see?' he said. 'Your kind of people.'

I cuffed him. 'Any more bright ideas like this and you're really in for it.'

The hall which had been fairly empty when we first came, was slowly filling up. You could spot them all: the intellectuals in leather chappals and long cloth shoulder bags, the aged rockers with carefully frizzed hair now thinning (like Handel on a bad hair day), the young stockbrokers in loud ties and pointy shoes. The musicians arrived and spent the next half hour tuning up. Random technicians approached the mike, said 'Testing, one, two, three,' then disappeared never to be seen again.

'And you?' I asked after a while. 'No girlfriend?'

His eyebrows rose. He looked at me speculatively, in silence. 'I bat for the other side.'

'Myrna?'

'She doesn't know,' he said quickly. 'I would thank you to keep it that way.'

'Of course, your secret's safe with me. It'll cost you though.'

'Drink?' he said, changing the subject. He went over to the bar—a table in the corner covered with a white cloth manned by two very bored-looking English girls—and brought back two cups of white wine. Warm, sweet, disgusting.

After four more of these, and some sporadic conversation held with difficulty over the baila music, there was still no sign of any food. I was quite ready to go home but Janak restrained me.

'If you go now, they will take it as an insult. They'll never forgive you.' His voice was slurred, the wine beginning to take effect.

'They?'

'The Louis Fan Club.' He giggled. 'They've already entered your data into their programme. A short list of ten eligible London girls will pop up on the screen any moment now.' Just then the music stopped, and in that inexplicable way that it happens, silence took over the room, spreading rapidly from table to table like a cloud passing over the sun. People looked up expectantly.

A woman appeared at the door in a full-length mink coat, her luxurious black hair worn loose and waist-length, merging with the black of the coat in one gushing torrent. She was accompanied by a man young enough to be her son—though by their body language you could tell they were an item. He was extremely good-looking, in a miniature poodle sort of way. The woman turned as if she had reached the end of the catwalk, surveying the room. She had everyone's attention, and you knew somehow that she knew it too.

'She is definitely not on your shortlist,' Janak murmured.

'Who is she?'

'It's a long story. They say . . .' he looked around to see who was listening (no one was, their attention being all on the new arrival) '. . . they say she's a very high-class hooker.'

'Sri Lankan?'

'Of course. They say she has members of the Royal Family on her list.'

I couldn't tell whether he was proud of this fact or disgusted. A bit of both, probably.

'So why is she here?'

'You mean because Buckingham Palace this isn't?'

I nodded.

'Beats me,' he grinned. 'Maybe she's looking for you? Her Mr Right? I can get you her number if you like.'

'Really?' I was thunderstruck.

'She's my aunt. Actually, my ex-aunt,' he corrected himself. 'My uncle is a doctor back home. Janine used to be married to him. Till she moved on to better things.' He then looked at something behind me and said quietly, 'So I won't have to get you her number after all. She's coming over.'

He stood up. 'Auntie Janine! What a surprise!'

'Less of the "Auntie", please,' she said, throwing her head back and laughing. She had a pleasantly husky voice, but when she laughed she hit various high notes. It was faintly disconcerting and odd. You found yourself laughing at her laugh.

'And who is this? I could do with a bit of this,' she said and began fingering my biceps. (The miniature poodle wrinkled his nose in faint disgust. I was very afraid he might cause a miniature puddle on the floor.)

'This is Louis' son.'

'Louis? That old fraud?' She began to laugh again.

I could have thrown my arms around her and kissed her when she said that. She opened her diamanté clutch bag and fished out a pen and scrap of paper, on which she wrote down a number. 'Get in touch with me, Louis' son,' she said. Turning around she walked off, the toy poodle trotting in her wake. She had not bothered to ask my name.

'You see?' Janak said happily as we walked home. 'I told you we shouldn't leave too early.'

*

I spent the next few days opening a bank account, registering at the local job centre, buying bed sheets and towels, laying in supplies. Janak's plumber, a young Irishman called Sean, came round to connect the gas to the cooker. He looked at the bare room with the two beds in it, the cooker standing between them like an overgrown bedside locker.

'You're cooking in the bedroom?' he asked in disbelief. 'Where's the kitchen?'

'Oh, the cooker's not for cooking,' I assured him. 'At least not for the moment.'

'Then?'

'I'll light it every night before I go to sleep. For warmth.'

'Sleeping with your head in the gas oven?' He shook his head at this inscrutable Asian folly. 'Have a nice life. What little you have left of it.'

'I promise I'll be careful.'

He looked at me for a moment, weighing his words, then grinned. 'I know they say the only good Indian is a dead Indian, but this is ridiculous!'

Telling that half-dead joke to a half-dead Indian endeared him to me more than anything else. Even more concerned about my dodgy lifestyle was the landlord Mr Brown.

'Awrright, boy? How you getting on?'

'Fine thanks, Mr Brown.'

'Quiet enough? They not bothering you?'

'They, Mr Brown? Who do you mean by "they"?'

'That fine then. That just fine!' He wheezed off gently like a ghost, deep into the bowels of the downstairs, and soon I heard the canned laughter of the telly in sharp nervous bursts, muted and mechanical.

I did not know it then, because reading newspapers was alien to me—the sort of thing that wrinkly grown-ups like my father did—but Margaret Thatcher had just come into power a few months before and the effect of her radical changes of policy was just beginning to be felt. In a few years, real estate was to become the national obsession, the Tulip Fever of the 1980s, the fallout of which would be felt for probably another century or more.

These streets of Brixton houses were about to change drastically, becoming so gentrified as to be unrecognizable. The black inhabitants of the Windrush generation would be replaced, for better or worse, by young white professional couples. It was not for us to debate the rights and wrongs of this subtle ethnic cleansing, planned or otherwise. We were only the builders—unwitting agents of this change, forming no part of the change itself. We were outsiders, Irish for the most part, and this single Asian, me. Those who took their place—'yuppies' as they were fondly known—were lovely young girls in white shirts and flat golden sandals, called Verity or Constance or Honour, and young men in stripey school blazers driving red Porsches. Every girl looked like Princess Diana, though not every boy looked like Prince Charles. All this to come: the Golden Years of Brixton.

7

'I'm afraid you might have to wait,' Father Mahesh said apologetically. 'Confessions don't start till 5.30.'

'Oh, I'm not here for confession,' I said, hastily sitting up. I was at the back of the church, in the last pew. There was a slight give to it—I noticed it was being ferociously attacked by termites. Father Mahesh gave me a quizzical look and padded off into the gloom of the nave. I hadn't sighted the place for half a year at least and he knew that. So, why now?

My father's operation was scheduled for the next day. What had brought me here now, to this church, I really did not know. It was comforting to sit in the dark, away from the procedures and upheavals, the daily ebb and flow of fresh crises. Inside the church they were still present, but faint—the sound of waves heard from a hundred yards inland.

The church had been beautiful once, with a marble altar rail and carved wooden altarpiece that I remembered from childhood. A well-meaning architect had removed all that in the interests of modernization; in their place a hemispherical white construction inset with a smaller golden orb housing the sacrament, resembling nothing more than a giant white breast with a golden nipple. There was perhaps some deep symbolical significance to this; but all I could remember were the sniggers and lewd comments made by the street toughs from the tenements nearby, who unaccountably attended Mass every Sunday.

In the silence I sat and thought: *How different my life might have been under different circumstances!* I knew now that I had to escape from home if I was to make anything of it; even if this meant starving in a slum. Perhaps I had known this all along but never had the courage to face up to the truth squarely. The irony was this: now that I was almost ready to make the jump, I couldn't. *Who would look after my father?* I doubted if any of the Satellites could be persuaded to move in at this late stage. As for my father, he would have growled and roared at any such suggestion. ('Are you out of your mind, Sanjay? To be looked after by a bunch of clucking poultry? I would rather die!') And it would be no empty threat; he was quixotic enough to follow through, starving himself in a fit of rage at the indignity of it all.

I sat there in the gloom a long time, shipwrecked, bobbing all alone on this wide ocean, hostile and unforgiving. And if there was any voice speaking to me from up above, I don't think I heard it. 'Please God,'

I prayed. 'Let him get well enough. Well enough so that I can leave him to start a new life.'

*

Who would have thought it? The operation is an unqualified success. Nobody has told us this: we have to work it out for ourselves. My father is warded in a rather smart wing of the General Hospital displaying, disappointingly, none of those Hogarthian scenes of picturesque squalor we have always assumed to be the very essence of the Gen. Hos. Only one small detail—and I hesitate to mention this because it sounds so churlish on my part—is the lack of a normal loo. Instead, there is a hole in the ground into which if you peer, you will see caverns measureless to man.

'Please,' I say to the nurse, 'could I please ask you to assist my father when the need arises, because he is too weak to squat?'

'Me?' she replies outraged. She raises herself up to her full five-foot-nothing height. 'Certainly not! You will have to do it yourself.'

So for the next three days I become a sort of glorified lavatory attendant. I cannot now remember if there was a spare bed for me in the ward or whether I slept on the (admittedly clean) floor. Thirty years later and I find I have quite blanked out these delicate housekeeping details from my mind.

Four beds down is a patient shackled by one leg to the iron frame of his bed.

'One of the better classes of jailbird,' my father explains. 'VVIP. If you have any influence at all in this benighted town, you get yourself transferred immediately from prison to the Gen. Hos. Better ambience for sure; though I can't imagine the food's much better. The leg chain is a small price to pay. In fact I think they only did up this wing to accommodate these VVIPs, so we have to be thankful.'

My father and I watch this important man for a minute. He lies on the bed, his hands folded prayerfully on the enormous mound that is his stomach, looking moodily at the ceiling.

'Probably planning his next big drug deal,' my father whispers loudly.

'Shh!' I hiss.

When my father is discharged, we are given terse instructions to see Dr Jayaweera the oncologist, whose practice is in Dehiwala. Another day, another doctor, another part of the city.

'See Colombo and die,' says my father. He looks at me sideways, slyly, to see if I have got the joke.

It is not funny to me. 'Shut up,' I reply. 'You sick fuck.'

That night, long after my father has gone to sleep, I climb up on a chair and take down my suitcase—cardboard and brightly coloured—from the top of the almirah. I get an old rag and clean it thoroughly, inside and out. It will not contain much, but it doesn't have to. I never had much to call my own. I push the empty suitcase under my bed. I have enough time to plan precisely what I will put into it. I am the pregnant woman who packs her bag months in advance because you never know, do you, when the baby might come?

*

Dr Jayaweera's surgery is on one of those leafy lanes that run down from Galle Road to the sea.

'Now that the cancer has been successfully cut out, we must zap the area to destroy any remaining cells,' he explains. 'So it doesn't come back.'

'I like a doctor who uses words like "zap",' my father says loudly to me.

The doctor ignores him. 'I want you to come to Maharagama twice a week. Alternate doses of chemo and radio. We won't take any chances.'

'When?'

'Tuesdays and Fridays. Starting tomorrow.'

My father rises to his feet. 'Come, Sanjay.' He motions with his fingers. 'Come, come. We mustn't keep the doctor waiting. He has a whole roomful of patients waiting outside.'

At this point, neither of us has any idea what this will involve. If we did, we would not be so chipper.

*

There was a house being renovated around the corner on Sandmere Road, which I passed every day. I was admiring it from the outside when a small man silently materialized by my side. He was smoking a cigarette. 'Want to look inside?'

I nodded.

'Follow me.' He ground his cigarette under his foot and *skipped* inside; there is no other word for it. He was incredibly light on his feet. Later when I got to know him better, I realized he had a whole repertoire of music hall numbers that he sang with a very professional lilt to his Cockney tenor voice. More than once I caught him leaping into the air and clapping his legs together, the way they did in those old musicals.

'Ernie's the name. I'm the painter and decorator round 'ere. Cup of tea?'

While the teabags were steeping, he took me on a tour. The upper floors were almost finished though work had not begun downstairs. I marvelled at how makeshift it all seemed to be, the instant-coffee-powder quality of the whole thing. The walls were not brick and mortar as at home, but stud partition: three-by-two-inch pine timbers with sheets of plasterboard nailed on. Ernie's job began at this point. His rolls of woodchip paper were pasted directly on to the plasterboard, gritty and coarse, covering up any deficiencies in the carpenter's work. Quick, cheap, easy—entire walls up and decorated in the space of a day.

I stepped with fascinated disbelief into this world of the instant house, the very antithesis of all those houses I had left behind in the old country. The most ingenious part was how, with just one stud partition, you could convert a two-floored house into two flats, a three-floored one into three. Since all houses were built to the exact same Victorian design, it seemed to me you could do this in your sleep once you knew how. I took to hanging around that Sandmere site for hours on end when I should have been out looking for a job. There was something about creating these new volumes out of the old that appealed to me greatly, this radical distortion of space using matter.

I had always had something of an aptitude for maths. Its truths seemed to me cut in stone—absolutes that had always existed, simply waiting for you to discover them—unlike science or religion or philosophy whose truths were more often than not found to be restricted by time and place. I loved mostly the quirks and oddities of maths, those facts not fitting into the logical scheme of things; perhaps because I was a quirk and oddity myself, never logically fitting in anywhere.

There was the Möbius strip, for instance, that you formed by taking a long flat strip of paper and twisting it once before sticking the two ends together, forming a sort of buckled wheel. If you then took a pair of scissors and cut this wheel lengthwise, along the middle, you ended up with two entirely separate wheels. So far so logical. What you did not expect was to have those two wheels inextricably looped like two links of a chain. I found this fascinating, though the sad fact was that no one else did. Nine people out of ten would find this stunning result irrelevant and immaterial. And exquisitely boring. It was not their failure to grasp that saddened me, it was their boredom. It only confirmed what I already knew—how truly odd as a human being I must be.

*

'Meet me for a drink this evening,' Janak said. 'Time you met the other half. You know The Swan opposite Stockwell tube?'

I shook my head.

'Straight up the road from Clapham North. Can't miss it. Eight o'clock.'

It was interesting how the demographic changed as you walked north up Clapham Road, changing from black working-class to white working-class as you neared Stockwell. In the pub there was lively Irish music playing. I was early. Getting myself a pint of bitter I settled into a corner to observe the regulars: the wizened Irish woman who sat by herself with her pint of Guinness and a chaser of vodka in a slim tall glass; the young couple who nursed their halves of cider all evening; the tattooed hard men from the surrounding flats, with their equally hard, equally tattooed women. It was a great place for solitary people: you could sit by yourself lost in the music and the smoky buzz of that room and not feel isolated. Just before eight Janak came in. With him was a Mediterranean man, muscular and compact, so swarthy that he was almost my colour. Leaving him to fetch the drinks Janak came over to join me.

'Is that . . . ?'

He nodded. 'Won't last though,' he said gloomily.

'Why's that?'

'Doesn't like the way things are at home.'

'Must be tough for him. All those illegals wandering around in their underpants.'

He grinned. 'You idiot! Actually, the problem *is* the illegals. They give him a lot of grief.'

I was puzzled.

'You have to remember how conservative they are. Coming from the deeply rural Sri Lankan south, or the traditional-as-hell north. In their eyes, we're the perfect example of sinful Western decadence.'

'But working illegally and cheating the establishment is fine of course.'

'Of course.'

'So that's why.'

'That's why what?'

'That's why they weren't speaking to me either. They thought I was your . . . Oh God!'

He laughed. 'Oh, this is George,' he said, introducing his partner who had just come up with their drinks. We spent the evening getting mildly tipsy, George and Janak regaling me with stories of various sexual encounters too salacious to repeat, outdoing each other in their efforts to shock this hopelessly provincial Sri Lankan fresh off the boat, the music swirling around us in a protective drunken haze. Inebriated as I was, I realized how far removed was this Janak—clear, open, unfettered—from the one Myrna knew, and the sheer impossibility of the two personae ever being reconciled.

*

Next morning I came downstairs to find Mr Brown wheezing quietly at the newel post. He handed me a letter, a thin couple of sheets in an airmail envelope. It was from Rani.

I had left the house in charge of the Satellites, to be used as a sort of clubhouse in my absence. Rani, who lived in the suburbs with a difficult daughter, or so she said—though it actually may have been the other way round—had volunteered to move in, occupying my father's room. She was also in charge of collecting rents from the Moratuwa tenants.

'Use it for your upkeep, your expenses,' I said. I knew that Rani was not well off. Besides, it pleased me to think that the house would continue to function as it had always done under my father's tenure, that it would be lived in, used. I knew only too well how a house in the tropics closed up for even a fortnight could become blanketed with damp, the brick dust tendrils of termite waste creeping up the walls even as you watched, like the leaves of some poisonous red jungle plant.

Rani said in the letter that everything was fine, that please, I was not to worry at all. (She would have been rather shocked had I told her the truth, that I had not given Colombo a moment's thought since I got here.) The tenants had been exemplary, even making the trek from Moratuwa to Colombo to pay the rent unprompted. Strangely, there had been none of the usual complaints. (Perhaps they were feeling sorry for me. Now that they had lost their one worthy adversary—I was not up to the mark, clearly—there was no more need for battle.) Myrna, Phyllis and Kamala dropped in virtually every day and they were all having such a great time, so bless you, Big Feller, for having made all this possible!

The letter ended with a postscript.

'It has come to our notice,' Rani wrote, 'that you have been seen consorting with that dreadful woman Janine Weerasinghe. Cease and desist, Big Feller! Cease and desist! (I chuckled not knowing where she could have dug up that antiquated legal phrase.) She has been known to break up marriages wherever she goes. (But I'm not married, Rani. I'm not married, am I?) She has great power over men. SHE IS A LOOSE WOMAN.' (This last phrase was carefully printed in block capitals.)

I put the letter away roaring with laughter. It was curious to think that even in those pre-email days news travelled at the speed of light. It was comforting to me that 5000 miles away, on an obscure tropical island, there existed a cabal of women watching my back. They had my best interests at heart: even if they were liable to get it entirely wrong much of the time. I loved them all, individually and collectively. I loved them the way other people loved their mothers.

I came out of my reverie to find Mr Brown still there, looking at me curiously with a new light in his eyes. 'What so funny, man, what so funny?'

'Nothing, Mr Brown. It would take too long to explain.'

'Well, enjoy it while you can because I giving you notice. You have to move out end of the month.'

Suddenly I wasn't laughing any more. 'But I only just moved in!'

'I put the house on the market yesterday.'

'What?'

'No peace, man. I don't get no peace. Too much noise.'

'I'm sorry, Mr Brown. Last night was my first night out. I was overexcited. I promise I'll be quieter from now on.'

He looked at me pityingly. 'It not you, son. It not you.' He wheezed away gently, leaving my new-found triumph, my cockiness, my supreme confidence completely incinerated.

8

I ran around the corner with this piece of news. I was let in by a rather hostile illegal who pointed silently upwards with a single finger. Or maybe he was just saying *up yours*. Janak and George were seated side by side on the bed looking glum.

'I hate to break up this festive mood with bad news,' I said. 'I've just been given notice by the landlord. He's selling the house.'

'You only just got there,' Janak pointed out.

'Spot on,' I said. 'Sharp.'

George just sat there looking crushed. *And I only just got the bed back*, he was probably thinking. Then he said something so obscure, so unintelligible, that it sounded like Greek to me. Which in a way was not surprising because he was Greek.

'Buy it,' he said.

'I beg your pardon?'

'Buy it. Can't be that difficult.'

'You need a mortgage,' Janak chimed in. 'You need a deposit.'

'How much would a house like that cost?'

'Twenty grand? Thirty maybe? The deposit would be 10 per cent of that.'

I already had that amount. Banked up the road at NatWest on the High Street. 'But a mortgage? How would I pay it back?'

'Split the house in two,' Janak said. 'Sell one half. Keep the rest.'

You know how it is when the hairs on the back of your neck begin to stand up and you realize there is something in the room? Something so monstrous and huge that you don't even need to turn around to know it's there. That is how I felt that morning as I stood in that attic, those two doleful faces in front of me.

'You're joking,' I retorted. 'It's the maddest idea you ever had.' But my mind was leaping on ahead, already on to the next move. And the next.

'There are plenty of houses around here for sale,' Janak commented. 'You don't just have to buy the first one that comes along. It's a buyer's market.'

They were both late for work. I left them to the mercy of the prowling illegals below and ran home.

'Mr Brown! How much did you want on the house?'

Mr Brown took off his hat and scratched his head. 'The agent knows.'

'Who's the agent?'

He looked at me puzzled. 'They'll be putting up a board soon,' he said after much deliberation.

I knew I was not going to get anything more out of him. It didn't matter. There were plenty of other houses. The more I thought about it the more compelling the idea became: like those tropical viruses that are just a suspicion of an ache in the morning—and by lunchtime you are shivering and sweating at the same time, and whichever way you turn there is no rest for you.

*

I found myself tramping the streets of Brixton and Clapham, collecting photocopied sheets of house details from any and every estate agent I could find. There were many. I was looking at anything between fifteen and thirty grand. I knew I could not deal with external structural issues; the bank would probably not lend on anything structurally unsound anyway, so the more viable properties were the ones at the top end of that range. I soon learnt the arcane language of estate agentese. 'Mature garden' signified a small paved backyard with a single tree. 'Needs work' usually meant that the rear wall was pot-bellied with subsidence. If it said 'light and airy', you could be sure that the windows had rotted and fallen out. So naturally there was a lot of light. And air.

It was lunchtime when I hit Clapham High Street. By now I was staggering under the weight of a whole armful of particulars, none of them listing the house I really wanted: 23 Tintern Street. The next office I got to was so small that it was manned by a single woman, who looked vaguely Sri Lankan, seated at a desk behind which was a row of filing cabinets. She got up with a swish of skirt as I walked in.

'I'm looking for houses under thirty thousand?'

'Can do,' she said, looking at me over the top of her specs. She was in a longish skirt, her hair in a bun. I added to my file the two properties she presented.

'I'll go home, look at these and get back to you.' Then a thought occurred to me. 'By the way, do you have a listing for 23 Tintern Street?'

She thought a moment then shook her head.

'Might you be able to find out who does?'

'I can make some calls if you don't mind waiting.'

I sat down in the one leather chair by the window, next to a rather dusty monstera badly in need of water, covertly examining her while she was on the phone. There was something strangely familiar yet unfamiliar about her. On the third call she struck lucky.

'It's with an agent in Stockwell. I've made arrangements for them to send over details this afternoon. Twenty-five and a half thousand pounds.'

'Are they open to offers?'

'You could try. Don't you want to see it first?'

'I already have. I live there.'

She burst out laughing. It was then that I realized who she was—those oddly musical, unexpected high notes.

She removed her glasses and undid her bun. 'I'm very angry with you. You never called.'

'But I came in person. I'm sorry I didn't recognize you with your clothes on.'

She laughed again, such a joyous, unconcerned laugh that you couldn't help laughing along with her.

'Can you do something for me? Can you make him an offer of twenty?'

'May take a while because it has to go through the main agent. Do you have a number I can call you back on?'

'Only the landlord's. And we don't want him having a heart attack because his buyer actually lives with him. So please don't say!'

'Well you have my number,' she said firmly. 'Now you'll be forced to call me.'

*

I walked back down the High Street with her laughter still ringing in my ears. I felt light-headed, drained, as if I had just run six miles. I had made an offer on a house without having any idea of where the money would come from. I had the deposit, true, and perhaps some of the conversion costs. But the rest? As for Janine, who exactly was she? Hooker by Royal Appointment or Clapham estate agent? The two professions seemed to be mutually exclusive. I knew she liked me—she had made that very clear—but I had never had a girlfriend. I did not know where to begin. The fact that the Satellites were outraged added a certain spice to the curry mix. But first things first. I had to get this house before it was snapped up by someone else. And there was the small matter of the mortgage.

The next few days were a flurry of activity. Bilquis's shop became my office. I sat with her copy of Yellow Pages, making appointments with all the local banks. Then I went home and wrote out, in longhand because I did not possess a typewriter, my business plan and cash flow chart. It was fairly simple: the upstairs could be sold as a two-bed flat for virtually the same price as the whole house, which meant the downstairs one-bed was almost pure profit. Easy, I thought. They'd be fools to refuse me.

Mr Brown watched my comings and goings with great interest.

'How's the sale, Mr Brown?'

'Good, boy, going good. Pack your bags. Have an offer.'

'Oh?'

'Some Asian feller.'

'Will you accept?'

'Nah. Too low. He offer only twenty.'

'How much did you want?'

'Hmm. Maybe twenty-four?'

'You think he'll come up to that?'

'Dunno boy. Mean bastards, these Asians. Mean bastards.'

'Thank you, Mr Brown.'

I rang Janine from my office, sitting on a crate of tinned jackfruit, with Bilquis breathing hotly down my neck savouring the vicarious pleasures of this deal. 'Offer him twenty-four,' I said tersely and hung up.

From a second-hand shop on Acre Lane I bought a thin red tie. Suitably dressed I turned up next morning at NatWest Bank on the High Street. They were holding my deposit so it was my natural first port of call. I explained to the manager, Mr Nikolaos, my plan. At least he had the patience to listen to the full story before he began shaking his head.

'You have no regular source of income, Mr . . .'

'de Silva.'

'Mr de Silva. Get yourself a regular job, then we might consider you.'

'But if I had a regular job I wouldn't be able to work on the conversion.'

He shrugged apologetically. 'We have our rules.'

I was in and out of there in ten minutes. I nearly went back to Acre Lane to return the tie.

*

'Where you going, boy? All smart like that?'

'Oh, here and there, Mr Brown. Here and there. How's the sale?'

'He come up to twenty-four. I taking it.'

'Congratulations, Mr Brown!'

'He damned fool, that Asian. I trick him good. Trick him *real* good!'

'How, Mr Brown?'

'Because I happy with twenty-three. I very happy with twenty-three!'

'But . . .'

Chuckling, Mr Brown wheezed away to the ghostly comforts of his telly.

*

Having got a refusal from every bank in the neighbourhood, I began looking further afield: BCCI on Park Lane, Allied Irish Bank on Bruton Street, Citibank on the Strand. At Citibank, a beautiful girl with red hair, mellow as candlewax, came down to interview me at the reception. After the usual refusal—for which she was very apologetic and I loved her for that—she wrote down a name and number.

'Go and see him,' she said. 'He might be able to help.' I read the name. Mr Wilson, Charterfield Investments, 49 Stillington Street, Victoria. I had been to twelve banks so far, all of which had said no. Charterfield did not seem to be a bank. I wondered what exactly it was.

*

'Do you have a solicitor?' Janine asked. 'I need to put one down on this form, now that Mr Brown has accepted your offer.'

I shook my head.

'I have one I can recommend. Back from my posh days.' She wrote a name down for me. 'You may have to talk them into it though.' She filled up the rest of the form and I signed it.

'Good, that's settled. Now we need to celebrate!'

I didn't want to tell her that I was there under false pretences, that I still had no mortgage. She would probably drive me out of the office in disgust. But I was naive enough to believe that things would fall into place.

'It's your lucky day,' I said. 'Where would you like to go?'

'I finish work at six. Why don't we go across the road then?'

I looked through the plate glass window of her office to see what lay across. 'Golden Curry Indian Restaurant', it said in yellow blue and purple. Also red green and orange.

'Tasteful,' I said. 'Smart.'

She laughed. 'I just love it, don't you? Food's great too.'

I promised to pick her up at six.

*

So here we are. Sitting inside this emporium of food, this veritable discotheque of Asiatic nourishment with flashing coloured lights and badly painted murals of the Taj Mahal. Janine explains to me how virtually every Indian restaurant in London is run by Bangladeshis, and all of them from a single area called Sylhet; that this restaurant is no different.

'I didn't know the Taj Mahal was in Sylhet,' I say, and she looks at me sharply to see if I'm taking the piss. Then she bursts out laughing and the owner who's pouring out our wine laughs with her, a big man with a broad face. He seems to know her well—she must come here a lot—and I wonder, does she bring her royals here too?

'By the way, they've been warning me about you,' I say. 'That you are . . . that you have other skills.'

'What? That I'm some sort of high-class tart?' She is scornful, and at once I feel mortified. 'That old story's been going around for years. Just because I don't spend my money on boring old houses in Surbiton like the rest of them, with furry carpets that smell of curry.'

'You buy full-length mink coats instead.'

She begins to tell me about her two difficult marriages, how each failed owing to her refusal to conform to what was expected of a good Sri Lankan wife. The second one was to a white man who still had definite views on how an Asian spouse was supposed to behave. 'You know what he said to me that very first week? "A woman's place is barefoot, pregnant and in the kitchen." So I gave him a slap.' She giggles. 'That threw him. Literally!'

'Then you walked out on him.'

She looks at me shrewdly. 'You really don't know much about relationships, do you? It was four long years before I walked out.

'I haven't bothered to divorce him,' she continues. 'We live apart.'

We are seated side by side on the cushioned bench that runs along the length of the restaurant wall. At this hour there are no other customers. She is wearing some sort of silky thing; every time she moves her thigh against mine it crackles, and the charge runs up my leg into forbidden areas.

The dinner is delicious too.

'So what made you come to this dump?' she asks.

Because you brought me here, I almost say. But that's not what she means. She means the country. 'I don't know. When my father was alive I led such an ordered life. He planned it, you know, I never had a say. Then he got cancer and all that order went to pieces . . . Now that the chaos has been let out of the box, I'm afraid it'll never go back in. I like the random accidental nature of this new life too much . . .' I take a gulp of wine, not knowing what has come over me. I have never said this much about myself to anyone before.

'So no furry carpets in Surbiton for you either,' she says and we drink to that. To our shameful lack of homing instincts. To that puzzling absence in us of the need for respectability; the need to establish ourselves at the table as major players of this strange new game called Find-My-Vernacular; the need, above all, to be whiter than white.

The restaurant has filled up and we are well into the second bottle. Her loud high–low laugh carries to the far reaches of the room. Under normal circumstances—or perhaps the pre-UK ones—I would be under the table by now, cringing, blocking my ears with my hands. Instead, I feel a sense of expansive proprietorship about that voice and that laugh. If the English punters don't like it they can go to hell.

'Where do you live?' I ask.

She looks at me mischievously. 'Up the road at Clapham Junction. A bus ride away.'

The unspoken request is there, the glove on the floor. I am being invited to pick it up. I should like to tell you that I do; in fact I don't. I am a virgin. I have never had a girlfriend before, let alone one old enough to be my mother. I am a coward. Where did they vanish, I wonder, all those free-wheeling principles I was just boasting about, the ones that might have enabled me to make the pleasurable esoteric choice here, instead of the boring furry one? I walk her to the Common and put her on the 37 bus.

I crawl back home, whispering to myself *Damn! Damn! Damn!* every step of the way.

9

You expect a lot of the High Level Road: the name sounds somewhat like 'The Stairway to Heaven', so you think, naturally, it must have been built to serve the needs of the very highest level of people. You could not be more wrong. It is full of tuk-tuks and ice-cream vans, young girls on bicycles and old men still learning to drive, vegetable vendors and oxen, all tussling for right of way. (Nowadays the oxen are no longer visible; perhaps because they are inside those jeeps, driving them.) My father and I are on our way to the hospital in Maharagama. Never having possessed a car we are on the side of the tuk-tuks in this War of Wheels, as we dodge and roll in between skittish school vans and murderous articulated lorries.

'Hah!' says my father, giving the finger to a black Pajero with tinted windows and flashing lights, as we pull ahead of it. He turns to me. 'If the cancer doesn't get you, the traffic will, eh, Sanjay?'

At the hospital, we find our way to Dr Jayaweera's office where he writes out a prescription for the chemo drugs we must buy. We walk through wards of bald-headed children seated on beds with their young mothers, and abandoned old people crying silently. At this time, there are no hospices in Sri Lanka where they can be hidden away, so they are all here: the dead, the dying, the hopeful, the praying. If you were ever tempted to feel that your life was valueless, with no meaning, this is where you would need to come: to realize the preciousness of the gift you have been given—its lapidary beauty, its gemstone brightness. So that you might remember once in a while to treat it less cavalierly than you do now.

On then to the rarefied world of the chemotherapy unit, furnished like the stage set of some abstract play. A single chair in a small bare room for my father, a single bench outside for me. The only decoration to be seen is a list—rather cavalierly scrawled in biro, hung on a nail in the wall—of the number of patients treated these past ten years. I notice idly that it has increased exponentially. *Is there an epidemic of cancer in Sri Lanka? Is it something in the food? Or is it simply that more people are being diagnosed?*

The nurse straps my father's bicep tight to make the veins stand out on his hand, then she inserts the cannula. The drug is injected with the drip. Not much different to the execution chair where the murderer sits while being administered the lethal injection. My father has a blank look in his eyes. *Where is he?* He is not with me. This too is a form of murder: the whole body slowly poisoned, in the hope of killing the few remaining cancerous cells in his throat. It is like spraying a whole field with Agent Orange to flush out the one or two Viet Cong cadres, who actually may not even be there.

At the end of the session he is barely able to walk. Every jolt of the tuk-tuk hurts his bones. For once in my life I long for the streamlined comforts of a big black Pajero, even one driven by an ox. We get home and he collapses on the bed. For the next two days he is unable to eat a thing. Next time I will know better. I will force a banana down his throat on the way to hospital, knowing that that's all the food he'll be able to keep down for the next couple of days.

His hair begins to fall out. He is a bag of bones and needs me to carry him to the bathroom every few hours, where he can only go if I turn on the taps. I have never had a child, but I know now what it is like. My father is no longer the fearsome man with the razor-sharp repartee, the withering put-down. The time for wit is long gone. All my life I have longed for the upper hand. Now that I have it, it seems I no longer want it.

The Satellites come around, bearing bowls of thambunghoda, a spicy broth guaranteed to scour your insides, the local remedy for all ills. My father shoos them away. Cancer is a journey you take alone, climbing steadily, looking neither to the left nor right. You do not know when you get to the top whether Death is waiting for you there, or whether it has continued further up. Sometimes what you think is your destination is only the base of the next mountain, one that was obscured from view when you began your climb. Death is having the last laugh. 'Ha!' it says. 'Fooled you again!'

So you rest awhile till you get your strength back. Your hair grows again, the flesh miraculously re-appears on your bones. But don't be fooled. It is almost time for the next climb. Death has only gone on ahead to change the bed linen, get the room ready for you.

I have never been one for the self-indulgence of grief. The white bed sheets laid end-to-end along the cemetery road, soaked with the crocodile tears of the entire village; the pipes, the drums, the practised shrieks of professional mourners, rising to a crescendo like burglar alarms every time you enter their field of vision: none of this does it for me. Grief to me is a dish best eaten alone, in a cold room. I realize that the warmth of the Satellites is only a temporary respite, one that will not last, so I shy away from the fire.

I am the man in the overcoat, who has just come in from the cold, who refuses to take it off knowing that very soon he will have to go back out again.

*

Charterfield Investments consists of two rooms off a side street in Victoria, up a slightly creaky staircase. The first thing I notice is a loose polystyrene tile hanging from the ceiling in the front room. No matter. I am not here to inspect building finishes.

Mr Wilson must only be a year or two older than me, but his tie—equally red—is a whole lot fancier than mine, the knot positively blooming in horticultural exuberance. He listens in good-natured silence to my spiel. By now I am fluent and glib with financial phraseology, practised and insincere. If all else fails, I know that I have quite a future selling potatoes and onions on the pavements of the Pettah.

After a while Mr Wilson silently motions for me to stop and retreats to the inner sanctum. He returns moments later with his boss, Mr Malcolm Jurisevicz, a large red-headed man with boiled-blue eyes, ferocious and unblinking. Mr Jurisevicz proceeds to shout at me. (And just when I thought it was all going so well!)

'Have you even built anything before? You realize that this is not a game for children? *Xkrrh*! How do you think you're going to pay the money back?'

I explain that according to my plan I have left aside exactly one month of interest payments. By the end of four weeks, I will not only have finished the conversion but also have found a buyer. Mr Jurisevicz's eyes pop out. His skin goes the colour of his hair. I am very afraid that he will explode; bits of red will get stuck to the polystyrene ceiling tiles and it will be difficult to scrape them off.

'Are you mad or just plain dumb? You Asians, you think you know it all, do you? Xkrrh!'

I do not know what 'Xkrrh' means in Polish—it may well be something as blameless as 'I need a pint of beer over here, and quick', but I am willing to bet it is not. After five more minutes of insult (and at least two more Xkrrhs), he says he will give me the money. Twenty thousand pounds of it. I cannot believe I am hearing this. The blood in my body stops pumping for a second. I feel like a torture victim whose feet have been systematically beaten for the last ten minutes with a wooden paddle, whose torturer suddenly leans over and starts applying moisturizer to them. I am overwhelmed with a sudden gratitude and unreasonable love for this hairy Pole.

But hang on a minute, there is a catch. The interest is 27.6 per cent per annum. The base rate at the moment is 14 per cent. I realize that by signing up I will become a sort of modern-day indentured labourer on a sugarcane plantation, or even a six-year-old carpet weaver from Jalalabad, whose eyes may at any time be put out by his owner for under-performance. But hey, I am Sri Lankan. I come from the most colonized country on earth. I am genetically hard-wired to take on slavery. After twelve firm refusals, this is as good as it is going to get.

'At the end of four weeks we will be sending our surveyor to re-inspect the premises,' Mr Jurisevicz warns. 'You'd better be ready by then.'

'Do you have a solicitor?' Mr Wilson asks.

'I do. I have not instructed them yet.'

'Well, get on to them immediately. We will issue the offer letter only after the searches have been done and the property valued.'

I ponder whether to say *Xkrrh!* as I leave, by way of thanks, but decide against it.

*

A quick sandwich and cup of coffee at the Kardomah Coffee House on Holborn and I am ready for the next appointment. New Square, Lincoln's Inn, could not be more different from the seedy environs of Victoria—with its rolled lawns, its mellow Queen Anne brickwork, its laid-back air of aristocratic insouciance. I am shown into the offices of Ambrose Appelbe Partners. In my enthusiasm I have come early, so I wait amongst the polished Chippendale, the freshly cut flowers, alone save for the discreet tick of a well-bred clock.

Felix Appelbe and Douglas Cooper are so expensively dressed, so soigné that I begin to feel uncomfortable in my shiny polyester anorak. I know now how the sugarcane worker must feel the first time he is sent up to the plantation house. If they are aware of my unease they are far too well-mannered to show it. In the gentlest possible way they grill me for the next half hour, a far cry from the methods of this morning's Polish Inquisition. They make me sign a cheque for a hundred pounds as retainer, and I am in business.

On the tube back from Chancery Lane I reflect how this whole enterprise rests on the successful outcome of so many variables, any of which might so easily fail. I cannot allow for them to fail. I must not allow even the possibility of failure to enter my mind. There is a sort of wish fulfilment at work here: it is dangerous to entertain negative thoughts; it pays to be blinkered and foolishly positive about these things.

*

'You know who's selling me the house?' I asked Janak. He looked blank. 'Your aunt.'

'Ex-aunt.'

'Whatever. You know she works just up the road from here on Clapham High Street? When were you going to tell me?'

He looked sheepish and defensive at the same time. 'Look, man, whatever you do with her is your business. Don't involve me. As far as we're concerned, she's trouble. We never had much to do with her after she divorced my uncle.'

'You were quite happy to introduce me the other day.'

'That just sort of happened. I had nothing to do with it.'

'Really?'

'Have fun. Don't get involved. That's all I'm saying.'

I wondered what he would have said had he known that we had already gone out on a date, that the cards were being shuffled even as we spoke, that my future was about to be laid out in front of me in two neat rows.

*

Mr Brown went out at four every afternoon to the Ex-Servicemen's Club on Acre Lane. At 4.30 p.m., when the coast was clear, I brought in Sean the plumber and the workers from the Sandmere site—Ernie, as well as Jo the chippie. Their electrician was going on to another big job, so he wouldn't be able to undertake mine.

'A weekend's work, no problem,' Jo said, giving me an estimate of 195 pounds for the carpentry work.

I made a face: only because that was what you did at home, never accepting the first quote that came along, believing that there was always room for negotiation.

'Suit yourself,' Jo said, and left in a huff.

Sean turned to me and wagged a finger. 'You shouldn't have done that.' He had himself quoted fifty pounds per bathroom and a hundred for the central heating.

'Who'll do the painting and decorating?' Ernie asked.

'I will.'

'What? You?' They fell about in merriment. I stood my ground, burning with embarrassment. I could not afford a painter. I had to attempt as much of the work as I could, only farming out the bits I was totally ignorant about. I had never painted anything before, let alone hung wallpaper. But that was not going to stop me.

'And the labouring?'

'Me again.'

They left shaking their heads.

The next stop was the Planning Department on Brixton Hill. There are certain people you are forever grateful to, even if you only see them half a dozen times in your life. Mr Whalley was one of them. He must have seen the callow youth in front of him, plainly no expert at any of the things he was so brashly promising to do.

'Draw the plan out on graph paper,' he said gently, 'showing the two units. Wherever possible, we encourage stacking—bathrooms on top of bathrooms, kitchens over kitchens. That way, the noises from your neighbour's flat upstairs won't bother you in the middle of the night.'

He helped me fill out the forms. The plans were passed in four weeks, giving me an inkling of how swiftly things moved in this marvellous country: so different from the courtly ceremonial dance of events back home, which proceeded at their own leisurely pace.

Looking back, I think with horror of all the things that could have gone wrong but didn't. I realize, cynically, how much of what happened was due not to any great skill on my part but to sheer damned luck. *Was there someone up there pulling strings, rewarding me in some obscure way for the horrors I had just left behind?* For whatever reason, here I was, like the goat in that Jaffna minefield—skittering across with foolish abandon, sublimely unaware of the dangers buried all around, the instant death awaiting it at every step.

PART II

10

It occurs to me that the central thread of this narrative—metallic gold, lucent, lending a certain brilliance and strength—is missing. This is the story of my mother. It is not that I have wilfully left it out. It is just that there is so little to put in. Running alongside the open-plan living room at home is a narrow corridor giving on to the two bedrooms, my father's and mine. It is full of the detritus of past lives: rolled-up carpets and out-of-date telephone directories, an elderly ironing board now unsteady on its feet and a floor polisher—bulbous and maroon—that no one has cared to use these past fifteen years. There is no natural light here and my father and I negotiate it every day by touch rather than sight. It used to be the stuff of nightmares when I was young—all those indeterminate shapes stacked against the walls, each with its own personality, poisonous and all-knowing, ready to strike as I ran across. Hanging here, where no one can see it, is a black-and-white photo of my mother. She does not look at the camera but away, in defiance, as if the photographer has taken the picture in spite of her protest. She is wearing a single strand of pearls around her neck and looks, as indeed they all did in the 1950s, like the Queen.

This is a person I do not know and cannot read: there are no markers in the picture that connect her to me, not even the familiarity of a background. It is a picture taken somewhere in England, at a time unrecorded, before she met my father. She is a subject on which my father—normally so garrulous—is strangely silent. It is almost as if the entire charade of his life has been put on display, carefully choreographed, so that my eye might be drawn away from this one salient feature: like the magician who flourishes his left hand so theatrically that you do not notice the card he is pulling out of his pocket with the right. Though in this case it is a card he is pushing back in.

There is just one story he told me years ago when he was a little tipsy, a little careless. I was three years old and my mother had taken me (my father did not accompany us) to see her family back in England, to their small manor house in Devon, in a village with the quaint and rather lovely name of Zeal Monachorum. When she arrived, her things were taken up to her usual room on the first floor.

Then my grandmother turned to look at the small child she was holding by the hand. Me. 'The piccaninny will sleep upstairs,' she said. Upstairs meant the attic floor, built into the eaves of the house, where the servants slept. My mother made her excuses and left the next day. She never went back to see her family again. When she died and was buried at the Bullers Road cemetery, no member of her family attended the funeral.

How much of her is in me? How many of my actions—irrational and random though they might seem—are directed by the unseen genetic machinery of this distant agency? I have thought about these questions time and time again. The clues, the entire filing system of this knowledge, must have lain dusty and unaccessed in my father's mind all those years. Now he is gone. *Why did I not ask him?*

The answer is one that makes me squirm. It is pride. As if I knew that he had control over this drip feed of fresh water that might have irrigated my dried-up existence. And he had simply turned the tap off. Asking him would have meant begging him to turn the tap back on. I was dependent upon his whims and fancies for so much in my life: all the day-to-day stuff I could perhaps have done without. But this other need was so central, so deep, that it would have been like begging him for eight pints of blood, which I was not willing to do. My failure to grovel abjectly on the floor haunts me to this day. *Was he waiting for me to plead?* Perhaps not. He was not a consciously cruel man. But he was an animal supremely aware of the power he exercised by way of control over this knowledge, the power he exercised over me. He was not about to give it up for nothing.

One day, they will find a method of compulsorily tapping into a person's mind before he dies, so that all the resources of his knowledge, the mineral-rich shoals and sandbanks of his experience do not go to waste—for all those quiet people who knew so much but volunteered so little; and of course for my father, who volunteered so much but kept back the one narrative that was so important to his son's life. The story of his mother.

*

Mr Brown's brother arrived in an ancient black Rover to take him off to the suburban splendours of Guildford, leaving the inner city to the likes of me.

'You not gone yet, young man?'

'I'm packed, Mr Brown. I'm paid up till tomorrow. I have one more day.'

He wagged his finger in reproach. 'The agent, she come today. She want the key today, you know.'

I was saved by Janine's arrival.

'Where the buyer?' he asked suspiciously.

'He's here, Mr Brown.' She laughed, a belly laugh hitting all the high notes. 'He's here. Then again, he's not here.'

Mr Brown's brow cleared. 'The buyer one of *them*, is he?' He nodded wisely. 'Oh, now I understand. Well, they can make all the noise they want now. I got the money. I out of here.' With a cackle, he got into the Rover and his brother stuffed the last of the oversized black bags on to his lap.

I waved goodbye to what I could see of him, the crown of his scratchy felt hat.

'So now you're the proud possessor of a London house,' Janine said. She couldn't keep the irony out of her voice. 'That old fraud would have been proud of you.'

I was curious. 'How did you actually know my father?'

'You won't believe this. He was proposed to me.'

'What? You're so much younger!'

'I was considered a whole lot of trouble those days. I smoked. I drank. I ran around with boys. I was *fast*.' She paused, reflecting. 'You know the classic Sri Lankan solution to that? Get them married off, and quick. I was eighteen. He must have easily been twice my age. They probably thought an older man would give me stability.' She laughed. 'I would have run rings round him.' She handed me Mr Brown's keys. 'Anyway, must get back to work.'

'Do you know of any electricians you can recommend?'

She thought for a bit. 'The Mulrooney brothers.' She wrote down their number. Then she gave me a peck on the cheek. 'Call me.'

*

I spent the morning hurling Mr Brown's junk into a skip. I wondered what he had actually taken with him because most of it still seemed to be in the house. The junk shop that sold me the beds came around and cleared a lot of the heavy furniture. By the end of the day the skip was piled artfully high, like a sort of gigantic amateur flower arrangement.

I went back to the Sandmere site to beg Jo to do the carpentry work.

'You're sure 195 pounds is not too much for you?' he asked, his eyes crinkling with amusement.

I apologized profusely. It was a novel experience for me—after a lifetime with my father—dealing with people who meant precisely what they said, no more, no less. He arrived that evening after regular work with his bag of tricks, his skill saw, his drill, his toolbox. The banisters came off immediately. Within two hours the stud partition was up.

'Have the eight plasterboards delivered tomorrow. I'll come by in the evening to finish off,' he said.

I went to sleep that night with the sawdust of slightly sweet freshly cut pine in my nostrils, a smell that instantly evokes, even now, that day all those years ago: the first day of my life as a builder. I wandered around for a while in the dark, the changed internal geometry of the house warping my perceptions, messing with the mathematics of my mind, in a way that was far more effective and exhilarating than any hallucinogenic drug. If Mr Brown's ghosts were around that night, noisily celebrating his departure, I was way too tired to let them spoil my sleep.

The subsequent days were spent at the timber yard, the plumbers' merchant, Moore's Builders. At the plumbers' merchant—all the way at the other end of

Ferndale Road—I asked the Asian-looking man at the counter, 'Excuse me, where are you from?'

'I'm from here.'

'Where are you really from? Originally?'

'I was born here,' he snapped. 'I'm British.'

I had fallen into the classic trap of so many people in the '80s, assuming that no black person could be British. I myself was not white. I had only asked hoping the man might be Sri Lankan, that he would throw his arms wide open saying 'I am from Galle or Jaffna or Kurunegala'. He never forgave me, treating me with surly contempt every time I went back.

All in all, I had a lot to learn about this world, but with the enthusiasm of the novice I learnt fast. It was a world into which I sank comfortably, gratefully. After clearing the house of all unwanted junk I set to work with a crowbar, ripping up the carpets. The worst of it was in the rooms where the foam of the carpet was stuck to the floorboards. Those patches took hours of patient scraping to dislodge. In other rooms there was newspaper underneath, saving me a lot of trouble.

Janak and George came around, settling into a corner cozily to watch while I worked.

'So it's the Sri Lankan method, is it?' I asked. 'Five men watch while the sixth does the work?'

'You're lucky we're even here,' George informed me. 'Janak has allergies.'

'Is that an allergy to dust? Or just work?'

'Oh fuck off,' they said good-naturedly. But they made no move to help.

Janak pulled out a paper from under the carpet. 'Look, the abdication of Edward the Eighth!' The King was on the front page with his abdication speech, easily the most handsome of the royals. '1936. This'll be worth a lot of money one day.'

'Your mother was English, wasn't she?' he continued. 'Myrna told me. That means you must have English cousins here?'

'I guess. My mother was estranged from her family.'

'You wouldn't like to make contact?'

'What's the point? What could I possibly have to offer them? What on earth would we have in common?'

The emotion in my voice must have been manifest. He put his hand on my shoulder. 'It isn't all about what you can offer them, or what they can offer you,' he said quietly. 'It's about just being; and the being that you are becoming apparent to those around you. It's no accident that the word contains both meanings.'

'Blah, blah, blah,' I said, annoyed. 'You're beginning to sound like my father.' I had always been a loner unused to outsiders analysing me, taking the liberty of making value judgements. It might have been all right, just, for the Satellites or my father to pass comment: I had grown up with them, they did not count. Anyone else made me uneasy. I had come to this country as a stranger free of all ties. It left me unfettered to reinvent myself. I did not want this existence qualified too soon, the drops of the old tincture tainting the clarity of the new. It was *becoming* I sought, not *being*.

He realized he had hit a nerve and changed the subject. 'What news of Janine?'

'Nothing really.' This was half the truth anyway. I omitted to mention that I thought about her constantly, that I could not get her out of my head.

'Okay, so you don't have to give us the juicy details if you don't want to.'

'There's nothing to tell. Though I do feel that she is someone I really admire for striking out on her own, making a life for herself in this city as a single Sri Lankan woman. Couldn't have been easy. Anyone else would have run back home at the first sign of trouble.'

Janak looked at George slyly, smiling. 'He's smitten, isn't he?'

'So what if I am?'

'She's a free spirit, Big Feller. You think you can tame her? Boy, you're so wrong. Just when you imagine you have her where you want,' he looked up at the ceiling, his eyes clouding over, 'she'll let you down. She'll let you down real bad.'

'Of course you have to take your uncle's side. I realize that.'

'Maybe,' he said doubtfully.

*

I called up the number Janine had given me and hired the Mulrooney brothers, Ted and Pat. They were treated with the greatest suspicion by the other workers. Electricians, I realized, were a race apart, preferring to fly in the thin rarefied air that existed above the earthy space of normal blokes. Then there was the fact that the Mulrooneys were ardent royalists. At some point in their career they had worked at Buckingham Palace; they never let you forget it. Jo and Sean were both dyed-in-the-wool Irish Republicans, so there were undercurrents on site which I was only dimly aware of. Pat worked for the London Electricity Board (LEB) during the day. Since the LEB had to inspect the wiring on any site, Pat was in the marvellous position of having to pass his own work, issuing himself the test certificate. Shades of Sri Lanka!

Sean ripped out the bathrooms (if you could call them that) and for the next few weeks I was dependent on the outside privy, washing every day in a bucket of cold water filled from a tap in the cellar. For that extra-special spa experience I went to the Clapham Baths along with all the other tramps of the neighbourhood. Not the sort of world you could bring a woman into, though I found myself thinking of Janine a lot.

Ernie spent much of his free time on our site, making mugs of tea, singing his music hall songs. He himself was not employed by me though he had introduced me to many of the team. They were all curious: to them I was that rarest of species, the Asian builder. There were Asian shopkeepers, Asian landlords, Asian waiters. I believe that in Brixton 1980, I was the first and only Asian builder. I took to going around with

Sean in his beat-up '70s Volvo, the colour of polished chocolate, and we were a familiar sight on those roads. Years later I was told that we were known as 'The Paki and The Paddy'. It sounded like a pop group. Of all the workers he was closest to me, in both age and temperament.

'You married?' he asked.

'Nah.' I shook my head, too ashamed to admit I had not even got to first base. 'And you?'

'Two kids. Wife, of course.'

He couldn't have been more than twenty-two or twenty-three. This could so easily have been me had I been living in London.

Ernie, who made it his business to know everything about everyone, filled me in. 'Got a girl up the duff, didn't he? Had to marry her then. Papists,' he said disparagingly. 'What did you expect?'

*

The radio is less invasive than the chemo, I find. He copes better. We have been at this game for weeks now and come to terms with it. When he smiles, my father looks like a rather amiable skeleton in a comic revue. The smile itself is unseasonable, unexpected. A welcome patch of global warming in the winter of our discontent. We have finally mastered the routine—the banana, the tuk-tuk, the treatment, the collapse.

And then, and then: the doctor declares a truce. He holds up a white flag. My father is given the all-clear. Oh, and just when we were so beginning to enjoy ourselves!

We are the inmates of the asylum: newly released, blinking in the sunlight, turning this way and that to catch the untroubled breeze. We look at each other not knowing what to do. We have been set free to go back to the world above, freed from the subterranean tunnels we have been inhabiting these last three months. The house on Clifford Road looks odd now, seen through fresh eyes. We have to re-learn to love those dark unswept corners, those unwashed glasses on the table, that corridor of monsters.

11

The Satellites were ranged around the dining table. They sang in cracked reedy voices, solemnly looking up at the ceiling—as professional singers do when they try to remember a complicated score. They sang:

Happy birthday to you!
Happy birthday to you!
Happy birthday, dear Louis,
Happy birthday to you!

I sat there eyeing the Green Cabin chocolate cake and the Fountain Café patties and cutlets. It was not often my father pushed the boat out.

'We did it, didn't we, Sanjay?' He put his scrawny arm on mine and grinned like a friendly ghoul. The flesh on his head had worn away, the fine planes of his skull visible through parchment-tight skin, and he was almost totally bald. I knew it would all grow back, but I kind of liked the way he now was. I had come to grow quite fond of this extra-terrestrial I was cohabiting with.

'Nothing like a spot of cancer to make you appreciate the finer points of life, eh, Sanjay?'

'Sixty-two and not out, not by a long shot,' breathed Rani, not always known for her tact.

I said nothing. I was the traitor in their midst, the cardboard suitcase under my bed now stuffed to overflowing with worldly possessions, all ready for escape into a new life. My *tenement* life.

The phone rang and I hopped up to answer it. When I came back they were silent, heads bowed, mouths crammed with chocolate cake, listening to BBC like sinners at prayer.

'Who was that, Big Feller?'

'Oh, nothing,' I said. 'It's St Xavier's. They want us to come in for the post-op consultation. The final one. Next Tuesday, with a Dr Marasinha.'

*

My beautiful day. The 7.45 a.m. mug of tea before work begins in the blistering, opaque frost of early morning. The raucous gossip and good cheer of other sites, other workers, when we troop off to Mandy's Caff for that gargantuan mixed fry breakfast at eleven: all the stories of X's mistress and Y's girlfriend and the threesome Z had only last Saturday while the wife was away visiting her sister in Dublin. Fiction of a fairly high quality, as improbable as my father's, if not somewhat racier in content. Evening tea under a single grim light bulb at four o'clock in the sunless half-grey world of dusk, all seated in a row upon a scaffold board supported by paint pots at either end. The workers finishing at 5.30 p.m., leaving me to carry on into the night for the next few hours. Short days of action, longer nights of introspection.

It strikes me then, dramatically, what little I need to be happy.

Walking in the pin-sharp rain down the length of Ferndale Road with two bundles of copper pipe bouncing on my shoulders makes me happy. Unloading a dozen fifty-kilo bags of cement or twenty half-inch plasterboards from the lorry makes me happy. The happiness is somehow tied to the extreme physical hardship: the happiness of the ox tethered dumbly to its cart. I realize that within the physical confines of this circumscribed space—this self-willed deprivation—your spirit can soar if you only let it, a little winged creature, all clockwork noise and mechanical buzz. But the happiness is contingent upon the hard work, the hemming in. The converse is true too: how you might have the entire singing sky of the universe at your disposal but still be earthbound, crushed by the iron bands around your soul. I realize how clever we are at making excuses: for our inability to fly above our limited circumstances; how happiness might not always be dependent upon the premise of unqualified freedom or the imagined pleasures of a deserted tropical island.

*

My co-workers are curious about my age, where I have sprung from. There is no point trying to explain. My life up to now has been so removed from theirs, so alien and inexplicable even to myself, that there is no hope they will understand. How to explain our bookishness—my father's and mine—coupled with the merciless straitjacket of our poverty, and the cynical hopelessness of that previous existence? How to explain our simple inability to help ourselves? So I keep information to a minimum. I am growing a beard now, and with my coarse Brillo-pad hair uncut and wild, I look of indeterminate age. If asked they might say I am forty, maybe fifty. I feel safe, protected within this physical and intellectual disguise. Is my new-found happiness a direct result perhaps of this disguise, this evisceration of my previous personality?

Brixton streets in those days had the reputation of being the most dangerous in London. The notorious sus laws—where the police could take you in for questioning simply because they didn't like the way you dressed—were in force. Whether this made the streets any safer or merely upped the ante on the violence is questionable. When I walked home at night in my shapeless Oxfam clothes, with my loping labourer's stride, little old ladies would cross quickly to the other side of the road. I knew then that my disguise worked beautifully, and I rejoiced. It is a wonder that I didn't get hauled in for questioning. Perhaps the police themselves were not fooled.

My father, that raddled old snob, would have turned his nose up at the people of this little world I found myself in. They might not have had his education, but their homes were clean, their kitchens bright and airy, and they were not afraid of spending money. The furniture in their sitting rooms was replaced without fail every year. My parsimonious father would have been scandalized beyond measure.

*

In all this, my ally was Bilquis from the corner shop. All my ordering was done on her telephone. If it was an important call, I would load the machine with ten-pence coins, praying the pips would not go off while I was talking, to give the game away. Bilquis would be behind me, monitoring the conversation, breathing hotly down my neck, her earring tinkling in my ear. The kitchen had not been assembled yet, so dinner meant a slab of mild cheddar from her shop and a loaf of sliced white bread. Bilquis would throw in a tin of lychees or jackfruit pieces—her gift which I did not have the heart to refuse. In a quiet corner of my house was a growing mound of jackfruit tins.

She must have found me an object of fascination: the fool who struck out on his own, shunning the well-trodden path of shopkeeperism. It was not that she expected me to fail. She watched with the benign curiosity of a scientist with her favourite lab rat, wondering whether this rogue animal might be made to conform to accepted behaviour or not. For it was well known then that we Asians were not genetically hardwired to be builders. We had a certain sharpness of business acumen, true; but it was the sharpness of the trading floor, the minute increment, the bargain basement. Our minds were not large enough to encompass the volumetric entirety of a Victorian house. Was I aware of this view? I am not sure. I knew I was watched by everyone: with awe, with dread fascination, with curiosity, with contempt. There is no fool, they must have said, like an Asian fool.

I had cleared the house of junk—three skips worth (having been properly yelled at by the skip driver for outrageously overloading the first one). I kept back a pitch pine kitchen table; and a hairy, shiny, over-stuffed chair on short spindly legs that looked like a hedgehog dressed for a night out. Also Mr Brown's television. This last was on hire purchase, and a few weeks later they came around and repossessed it. Till then I fell asleep in front of it every night, watching '80s sit-coms with the ghosts comfortably ranged around me, all of us laughing dutifully at the punchlines when they came.

*

We are now two weeks into the job, with two more to go. The clock is ticking loudly in my head.

'Time to go shopping for bathrooms and kitchens,' Sean says. I am beginning to rely more and more on his choice and taste. The youngest of the team, he has clear ideas about what young people might look for in a flat. As for me, I am beyond help: back home, my father and I lived with the same kitchen and bathroom from the time I was born, indifferent to any changing fashions in plumbing.

If you are a student of history, you will be aware of the various high-water marks of civilization—the Age of Reason, the Renaissance, the Belle Epoque. If you are old enough, like me, you may also remember that the 1980s were the Age of the Avocado Bathroom Suite. (Not that I am blaming Sean for this choice; it was easy to be swept along by the avocado hysteria of the times.) It wasn't only avocado. There was Burgundy, Champagne, even Midnight Blue, for the chosen few. This last was particularly insidious: only after you had installed and started using it did you realize that you could never get rid of the white soap marks that appeared unfailingly on the drying porcelain. Then there were the kitchens from MFI, white with a thin red trim, so radical and cutting-edge at the time, so sadly passé now. I wonder if in some quiet leafy corner of London there is still a Mr Brown, living in solitary peace and contentment with his red-and-white kitchen. Once Jo had put the kitchen in I realized that I could not cook in it: the turmeric from the curry left indelible stains on the white worktop. So there I was, with a bathroom in which I couldn't wash, and a kitchen in which I couldn't cook. Never mind, it all looked smashing; just right for that trendy first-time buyer too busy to cook or wash.

It was time to start hanging the woodchip. I went up the High Street (I could see Janine hunched over a file at her desk) to the paint shop at the top, where I invested in a light folding trestle table, paste and paintbrush, and rolls of woodchip paper. Also several gallons of a particular emulsion called Disco, at 1.99 pounds a can, thin and transparent as French consommé. Then I made a second journey for a pair of aluminium steps.

I waited till the workers had gone home, preferring to make my mistakes in private until I got the hang of it. Sadly, this was not to be. Janak and George turned up. They had a sixth sense about this, turning up without fail every time I was about to make a fool of myself. I mixed up a batch of glue in a bucket and set to work.

'There's more glue in your hair than on the walls!'

'Come home, Big Feller, we'll give you a good scrub down!'

'Yeah, you'd like that, wouldn't you?' George muttered jealously to his partner.

I had only ever watched Ernie at work; he had made it seem so easy. Nobody had told me that you must never start at a corner, which seemed to my mathematical mind the logical place. I did not know then that quiet trick of tearing the paper irregularly to hide the join and cover any bulge in the plasterwork; that you must smooth away the air bubbles from the centre of the drop, never from the sides. By the time I had hung a few sheets I could see, even with my hopelessly crooked eye, that the drops were hanging at an angle.

George and Janak were hysterical.

'That's right,' I said in a huff, 'laugh all you want. Easy when you don't have to do it yourself.'

George got up. 'Let me show you,' he said grinning. He mounted the ladder and hung three perfect drops, effortlessly.

'You know,' I said, 'for a gay bloke your paper hanging is remarkably straight?'

He punched me on the shoulder.

'You wouldn't like to hang the rest of it?'

'No way. The pub's calling. Now that I've begun, I think you'll find it much easier.'

He was right. I promised to join them in a bit, knowing very well I wouldn't. For me, this was heaven: the yellow light on the extension cord, the slightly sweet smell of wallpaper paste in the bucket radiating its over-ripe warmth, the radio playing this week's hits; outside on Tintern Street black now with winter, the capped and coated figures of my West Indian neighbours hurrying home from work, one or two peering in through the sash windows at this strange spectacle. I know now that there are very few periods given to you when your soul opens up its lock gates to let in the happiness. The trick being to recognize these moments when they are granted to you, to rise easily upon the tide as it surges in, having first emptied the chamber that is your mind of everything else in preparation; to possess this flood then, the way you might possess the air upon entering a room—a room that is empty of all else but this oxygen; and of course yourself.

*

I walked across to Bilquis at ten, just before she closed, and picked up a slab of mild cheddar and a pint of milk.

'Just need to use your phone,' I said.

She watched me curiously from behind the counter. 'Who you calling?'

The phone rang a long time. I held the coin in the slot, ready to push it in.

'A woman, innit?'

I didn't answer. She began to shake her head with an air of finality.

'Not a good woman, innit, if she's out this late?'

'Well, you're not at home either, are you Bilquis?' I left quickly before she could think of a retort, marvelling at the intuitive powers of women—Byzantine, almost occult—and the corresponding simplicity of men, transparent as the pages of a nursery colouring book.

That night, I could not sleep. *Who was she out with, which royal client? Had she gone to the pub with friends? Wasn't it simple-minded and naive to expect her to sit in every evening waiting for my call?*

The old house creaked and groaned as it settled for the night. Then I heard it. A door closing below me and hushed muffled voices. I turned over. I must have fallen asleep at some point because I distinctly remember waking up again, briefly, to hear the canned laughter of the television downstairs.

12

So here we are at St Xavier's to *channel* (oh, how I loathe that word, redolent as it is of ether and antiseptic and the faintest smell of shit) the head of the cardiology unit, Dr Marasinha. He explains how, now that the cancer has been obliterated, he will set my father's heart straight, rejig it to the rhythms of a normal person. But when was my father ever normal? Why must his heart, which has ticked erratically these last sixty-odd years, now be made to march to the beat of a different drum? Why tinker with an old car that has been running happily all this time, however imperfectly? I ask Dr Marasinha these questions in my halting layman's English.

He smiles, a gentle philosophic smile that contains his unqualified forgiveness for my ignorance. I know you cannot follow me to the outer reaches of my stellar intelligence, it says. I do not expect you to, nor do I hold it against you. Just trust me. I will make your world better, for it is within my gift. I am the Doctor.

'Take one in the morning, and one again in the evening,' he says. 'That should do the trick.'

Let us call these pills Alpha pills, because drug companies have long, long arms, because even after thirty years they might decide to sue me. For all I know, these pills are still being prescribed today, with a by-now stupendous record for achieving the demise—so gracefully, so easily!—of all those patients prescribed their use.

'Your father,' says Dr Marasinha with his sleepy smile, 'will suffer a series of mini-strokes. He will slowly lose the capacity to lead a normal life. You must be prepared—how shall I put this?—to take over the living of his life on his behalf.'

The words are so poetic, so philosophically put, even if the rationale behind them is impossible to fathom. 'Why, doctor, why?' I ask distraught.

'I have already told you. So that his heartbeat can be regularized. We cannot take the risk of his heart giving out on him.'

'No. Far better to kill him off right now.'

'What's that?'

'Nothing, doctor.'

And with these kind words the good doctor waves his wand, the curtain goes up. To the sounds of a drum roll, the nightmare that is our very own comic revue—starring the skeleton that is my father and the great dumb sidekick that is me—begins all over again.

*

You will ask why I did not use my common sense and throw the pills away. It is easy to speak in hindsight. Far more difficult to take that decision with the full weight of experience and science against you. The Satellites were evenly divided on the issue. There were some like Rani who were with me on this. Against us were the more fine upstanding members of the cabal. Those for whom the word of a doctor was only just below the word of God. The deciding vote would have been my father's own: all his life he had had a reverence for Western medicine, an implicit faith in all drugs. He had always been a hypochondriac with a voracious appetite for pills. Had he been consulted his vote would definitely have been for the good doctor, and all of us knew that. So it was Alpha all the way. It did not disappoint. Within a month my father had had his first stroke.

Later in London I read an article, copied from the *Washington Post,* of the results published by two Danish doctors after extensive trials with Alpha. Their findings were that Alpha was a killer. This was something I knew already. You did not have to be Danish, or even a doctor, to come to that conclusion if you had lived with my father those last few months.

You will have heard of that most sophisticated form of murder invented by the Chinese, death by a thousand cuts. Alpha was merely an improvement on that, an entirely bloodless, hands-free variation of the method. Of course, when I say hands-free, I am being over-protective of your squeamish sensibilities.

I am letting you off the daily shit on the bed sheets, the food dribbling down his clothes owing to an inability to swallow, the bedsores blooming like red, red roses all over his back, each weeping slow tears of grief: all those details that formed part of my daily routine.

The Satellites rose magnificently to the occasion, willing to help with anything.

'They're *women*, Sanjay,' my father said. He did not want his privacy, his dignity compromised by those he had known in another life under more fortuitous circumstances, those he had bullied mercilessly when he had had the upper hand. Somewhere in the recesses of his stroke-struck mind was an awareness of the loss of face this new turn of events might involve. So, Sanjay must do the work. When he had the energy he screamed at Myrna or Phyllis, or whoever happened to be present, driving them out of the room. Sanjay knows best, don't you my boy? Sanjay is young, Sanjay is able-bodied. Let him do it. He didn't even like me conferring with the Satellites behind his back, thinking I might be giving away state secrets, undermining his authority in some way. So any conversation had to be carried out in whispers in the front yard. It was a small house. In his presence we were as quiet as penitents at a shrine.

The Satellites helped the only way they could, with limitless dishes of food. 'Eat up, Big Feller. You need to keep your strength up,' they said. I can in truth say that I was magnificently fed during this time, putting on pounds of flesh, thanks indirectly to Alpha. The

Danish doctors would have been immensely gratified had they known of this amazing side effect.

*

'So is this it then?' Janine asked, swishing her skirt and clip-clopping her way through the house, her first time back after selling it to me. Tomorrow my time would run out: the end of the allotted four weeks. I had asked Janine to come and give me an informal valuation before Charterfield sent its surveyor. She looked silently at my pitifully threadbare belongings—evidence of my wonderful new English life—laid out on the bare floorboards upstairs for all the world to see. I should have been embarrassed had I not been so nervous.

'So. What do you think?'

'Finish it first,' she said thoughtfully.

'But the two flats are separate and self-contained. There's only the decorating downstairs left.'

'Complete the work. Otherwise they won't believe you'll do it.'

I followed her downstairs to the bathroom, all cunningly in place though not entirely operational because the hot water was yet to be plumbed in. The Midnight Blue washbasin was proudly shouting out the victory of its white soap marks.

'Who did the tiling? A blind man?' She looked at me and laughed. 'Sack him. Please. Make sure he never works again.'

I silently swore never to tile another bathroom as long as I lived.

She went out to the backyard with its lone quince tree and looked up at the rear wall. 'The roof? The drains?'

'Yes, well,' I said uneasily. 'I'm sure they're fine.' I did not have enough money to tackle either roof or drains. I had to pray they would not let me down when it came to it.

'We can market the downstairs for fifteen and the upstairs for twenty-two. But don't even think of showing it till you're finished.'

Thirty-seven grand! Even after allowing for legal and agents' fees, after repaying Charterfield, I would clear over fifteen. I would be rich beyond my wildest dreams.

I saw her off and crossed the road to my office. With shaking fingers I dialled. Mr Wilson picked up, and I pushed in three ten-pence coins. I could not risk Mr Jurisevicz's ire by letting the pips go off in the middle of any conversation.

'The flats are ready for you,' I said proudly when he came on line. 'Send the surveyor. Do your worst.'

'I will,' he replied.

I hardly slept that night. There were the usual sounds from below; at one point, a loud crash. *Nerves*, I thought. I must get a hold of myself.

*

The surveyor arrived next afternoon in his silver Jaguar, clipboard in one hand, smoking cigar in the other.

I looked at his expensive tweed jacket, his polished nut-brown brogues, and smiled to myself. Not the sort of attire for climbing into attics to inspect roofs, nor for opening up manholes to poke about in drains. He left after five minutes, barely bothering to nod goodbye. I gave him an hour to get back to his office, then ran around to mine. Bilquis must have sensed my urgency because she came and stood behind me, listening over my shoulder, tinkling in my ear with every move of her head.

'Mr Jurisevicz, what's the verdict?'

There was a pause. I held my breath.

'You idiot!' he shouted. 'The surveyor says he's never seen such disgusting workmanship in his entire life. The flats are not fit for even *pigs* to live in.'

'Mr Jurisevicz, you don't have to be so insulting.'

'Insulting? I'll show you what insulting is if I ever catch you, you—'

'Mr Jurisevicz—'

'You *Asian*!'

'I know. Sorry about that.'

'We'll be foreclosing on the property, putting it up for auction. If you're lucky, you'll get something of your deposit back. Don't bank on it.'

'Mr Jurisevicz, please—'

'Please what?'

'Please give me four more weeks. I have the interest money. I promise I'll finish the flats and find buyers in that time.'

At this point there was an interruption at his end. Was Mr Wilson putting in a word on my behalf?

Mr Jurisevicz came back on the line. 'Four weeks. Not a day more.'

'Mr Jurisevicz, thank you, *thank you*! I promise you won't regret it.'

'Xkrrh!'

The phone went dead.

'Bastard pig!' said Bilquis. 'Who does he think he is?'

I hung up the phone, my hands shaking. It would be the end of my life in England. I was gambling everything on this one last throw. Double or quits. I could already see the dining table with the transistor on it, the looming dark corners. Just when I thought I had broken free.

I went around the corner to Bedford Road, my first stop in any emergency. I could smell the curry goat bubbling in the kitchen. Janak and George were in their room at the top as usual. Illegals in underpants prowled below, like lions on the Serengeti Plain, searching for goat.

I explained the situation, how close I was to the edge.

'Prick!' said George. 'Pole!' Having exhausted his superb fund of expletives, he fetched his remedy for such occasions, three large bottles of Strongbow cider.

'Myrna'll be pleased,' Janak said. 'She thinks you've got into bad company. Time to go home, get a decent job.'

'Like you've done?'

'Yeah, well. She gave up on me, didn't she? That's why she started on you.'

We sat there getting steadily more tipsy, the skylight a darkening rectangle above our heads, starless, joyless. Perhaps she was right. I could see my future in London in all its bleak glory unrolling before me: shift work in one of Janak's petrol stations, a bit of supplementary labouring on the side; cash in the hand, enough to live on halfway decently but not enough to revel in luxury. Before I knew it, I would be thirty—*oh my God, old!*—no good for anything else. That day, I silently vowed to myself sitting on the edge of their bed that I would not go back till I was thirty, however bad this new life was; and however good this new life might turn out to be, I would still go back at thirty, giving it all up.

'Stay for dinner?' Janak asked.

'Goat?'

'Goat.'

'Can't. I have stuff to do.'

'Yeah, right,' said George. They did not care either way. They had each other to fumble with in the dark spaces of their attic. They were self-contained, a fact I was painfully aware of.

*

'Take this filth away!' he roared at me. 'Who cooked it? It's not fit for cattle.'

'Myrna made it.'

'What did I tell you?'

'Just one more spoon,' I begged. 'Please. You have to keep your strength up.' I had been feeding him for the last forty-five minutes. He had eaten two spoons so far.

'Why can't you bloody let me die in peace?'

'Are you crazy? That's not how it works.'

'It's what you want, isn't it? I've been watching you. You can't wait for me to die so you can escape.'

Even through the fog of his pain and confusion he had somehow found his mark. Unbelievable. I tried inserting the spoon into his mouth. He brushed it away violently and the plate went sailing through the air. There was rice and curry all over the floor. Idly I watched one fat gout of turmeric gravy trickle down the wall. Getting up wearily, I went to fetch the dustpan and brush.

'Let's see how you manage without me,' he called out, with an air of grim victory. 'Bloody disaster, that's what you'll be. We all know that.'

I felt then an odd whistling in my head as if some sort of firecracker had gone off, and the rage inside me exploded into a thousand sparks. I found myself instantly by his side.

'One more word,' I hissed. 'Just one more word and I'm out that door and I'm never coming back. You understand me?' I was gripping the bones that were his arms, brittle as breadsticks. A little more pressure and they would have snapped.

'You're hurting me,' he said through clenched teeth.

I happened to glance into his eyes then and saw something that almost made me buckle at the knees.

The look of sheer panic on his face, the fear of being abandoned.

I didn't mean it, I didn't mean it! I wanted to beg. *Please, please forgive me!*

Of course, I couldn't bring myself to say it. I was even more proud than he was.

*

The days drove on, careering wildly down that one-way road. I was in control of a car with an empty fuel tank, the red light winking with a condescending air of finality. It was only a matter of time before we shuddered gently to a full stop. The strokes began increasing in frequency. It was heart-breaking to watch the corrosive acid of his wit neutralized in stages to the blandness of milk. His features, once sharp and all-knowing, became strangely smoothed-over, baby-like. The malicious glitter left his eyes. It was no longer the face of the stand-up comic but that of the puzzled tourist—who has accidentally strayed into the Republic of Alphastan, ignorant of its language, unsure of its customs.

I wanted the old old man back. *Return him to me, please God*, I prayed. *I'll never say another word against him. And you know what? I will not escape. I will stay at home and look after him for the rest of my life, even if it kills me. I promise.*

*

The Strongbow had begun to take effect. It was time for me to leave. I don't think Janak and George even noticed me go, so busy were they making a meal of each other. I let myself out quietly—down the cord-carpeted stairway, past the tobacco-stained walls—trying not to disturb the prowling underpanted illegals below. I cut through Tremadoc Road to the High Street, where the wind moaned and howled as it picked up speed on its way to the Common. The street lights were coming on. The day was dying, giving way to the mineral melancholy of the night. I looked up. *How immense this sky, how minute and inconsequential our existence!*

Most offices along the street were already shut. I could see her through the window, bent over the filing cabinet, putting papers away. I knocked. She looked through the glass and seemed surprised. She came to the door and let me in.

'Lock the door,' I said. 'Pull the blinds down.'

13

My father died today, Sunday, at 1.22 in the afternoon. I am all alone in the house. I sit there with him a long time. His presence is so strong, so overpowering that it feels like he is still with me, even if the body is gone. As far as I am concerned, the body left a long time back—when he sank into that gentle coma. Death, now that it has actually come, is only an infinitesimal lessening of an already near-zero state, the final bump along the bumpiest and slowest of dirt tracks.

Almost six months have passed since that first stroke. It may sound like a week in the pages of this book. If so, I apologize. I have waited thirty years to write this account, and till I do, I know his spirit will have no rest, so I am eager to get to the end. These words will put a full stop to the flamboyant and capricious novella that was his life. One whose pages we turned so cavalierly, never imagining for a moment that it would end so soon. In my hurry to finish this account I am rushing headlong, paying no heed to the events that lined my road during that horrific half year: a car speeding with full knowledge towards the crash that awaits it, at the unprotected railway crossing ahead.

Now that it has happened I am in that eerie space of twilit silence, the swimmer practising yoga moves on the ocean floor, the skydiver in balletic freefall, slow motion through the clouds. In a little while, I know I have to get up and restart the machinery—the doctor, the death certificate, the funeral arrangements, the almsgiving—all the panoply of rules decreed by law and good manners for your conduct, which exist only to take your mind off the main events of the day, your grief and your loss.

Myrna has left me a plate of yellow rice and chicken curry. I eat at the dining table with the silent transistor for company, and think back to the last conversation I had with him, if you could call it that, the many strokes having made speech nearly impossible. My father looked at me, and I could see the great effort he was making to squeeze some expression into his eyes. He got as far as mild mischief, not quite making it to malice.

'*Mmplchna*,' he said with a sigh. '*Nnghri*.'

I knew what he was saying. 'Montepulciano,' he was saying. 'Anghiari.' The perennial cry of the tourist who has not quite finished seeing everything; and now it is time to turn back for home.

I squeezed his hand. 'Of course we'll go,' I said. He had always been full of bluster. It was my turn now.

All his life he had held in his mind a booking for Tuscany. Alphastan was as far as he was ever going to get.

The body is next door in the bedroom. There are exquisite and nuanced rules for its disposal, but these are only a sideshow, a distraction. The car has crashed into the train: a twisted installation of crushed steel and glass that remains at the crossing, to be received with great gusts of grief by villagers rushing from their huts to the scene of the accident. Meanwhile the train speeds on, carrying with it the spirit, supremely disdainful of the wreckage it leaves behind.

Wearily I get to my feet and make my way down the road to Dr Nava. She returns with me—paying a house call for the first time in so many years (how my father would have crowed in victory!). She issues the temporary certificate I have to take to the Grama Sevaka. Because nobody is dead till the state officially declares them dead, and that is no easy task. If death fails to kill you the bureaucracy surely will, as my father might have said. She writes out her form and hands it to me.

'What will you do now?' she asks, the first of the fifty-or-so variations of this question to follow in the coming week. It is ironic. Now that he is gone, there is no more reason for me to escape. I am finally master of myself.

Dr Nava looks at the body and an expression comes over her eyes, one I cannot quite read. It is tender, quizzical, apologetic. 'So they got you in the end?' it seems to be saying. 'You really were as ill as you always said you were? I am so sorry we never believed you!'

When I come back it is dusk and the house is thick with Satellites (they all have keys now). Nosy neighbours and pariah dogs off the street have begun to breach our defences; also cartloads of nuns. Overcome with grief, nobody has the strength or hard-heartedness to repulse them.

Let the games begin.

*

I am under starter's orders again, with four more weeks to run. Having erupted gloriously from the blocks with what I fondly imagined was a winning performance, I have been ignominiously recalled. It was a false start. I had got it wrong. Now another chance, a reprieve of four more weeks. I don't know how lucky I am. In Jalalabad, they would have put out one eye already.

This morning on site, as we sit with our mugs of PG Tips strong as rust, nobody says a word. They all know that something has gone badly wrong. Afterwards Ernie takes me around the house, giving me a detailed list of what I can and cannot do to make the place more surveyor-friendly. I can see that it gives him a certain pleasure to point out how badly wrong I have gone. Never mind. In a twisted sort of way he means well, and I am grateful. The gutters and downpipes need renewing. I will need a two-stage ladder, and he recommends a local hire shop he'll take me to, where

I can rent one by the week. When it comes to the decoration, his eyeballs roll.

'There are certain walls where no amount of woodchip will help, son. You need a plasterer.'

The question is if I can afford one, given my fast-dwindling resources. 'Anyone in mind?' I ask nervously.

Ernie discounts Val or even Donal; their work may be better, but they'll be too costly. 'Try Douglas, son. He can be really good.'

'When is he not good?'

'When he's high, son. Which is most of the time.'

I come back with the ladder that afternoon to find an unsigned note slipped through the letterbox.

'I'll be home at eight. 13B Ilminster Gardens. Take the 37 bus from Clapham Common and get off by Arding and Hobbs.'

And suddenly, in spite of all the bad news, I am as high as Douglas. I even attempt to sing as I make a start on the downstairs.

The Mulrooneys eye me moodily. 'You ought to be on the radio,' they say. 'Then we could turn it off.'

At 5.30 p.m., as soon as the others pack up and leave, I stop work. I go to the Baths where I stand under the hot shower for half an hour. Under normal circumstances this would be the deliriously high point of my pampered evening of spa treatment. Tonight it is only the first course.

I have promised to meet Douglas outside the Sandmere site at seven. When I walk back he is already there, a tall and rangy Jamaican with the most exquisite old-world manners you ever saw. I walk him around the corner to Tintern and take him through the house, pointing out the precise walls that he needs to plaster—not too many since I need to minimize costs.

Douglas raises his head and listens. 'Is anybody else here?'

'Why? Can you hear something?'

We both listen. There is only silence. 'An old house settling,' I say with a laugh. 'Ghosts.'

Ten minutes after he leaves I leave too, in my Sunday best (my only best), armed for action with those little squares of silver foil without which no young builder's life is ever complete.

*

Arding and Hobbs is a splendid Edwardian Baroque palace, a *grande dame* of a department store. Janine lives in the street behind, on the first floor of a Victorian house. Again, I am surprised. I expected something low-slung—all steel and glass and horizontal—to match the horizontal inclinations of this royal courtesan (oh, how that false and unfair reputation lives on, and how I love to fantasize about it!). But no. It is the last word in pink: pink curtains, pink carpet, dusky pink sofa. Against one wall is a glass cabinet filled with Clarice Cliff pottery in confectionary colours good enough to eat. It is the most feminine room I have ever seen, which is surprising because I realize that Janine, when you get to know her, has the personality of a man. She thinks like a man, she acts like a man.

'I have my needs,' she declares in her high-low voice, with her high-low laugh. 'And I'm not afraid to act on them.'

'Is that why they're so afraid of you?'

'How they fear me!' There is a note of glee in her voice. 'They'd lock up their husbands if they could, when they see me coming.'

On the table is a large glazed earthenware pot of boeuf bourguignon, lit either side by two pink—what else!—candles. 'Men are like motor cars,' she says simply. 'You have to put in lots of petrol to get maximum mileage out of them.'

In the adjacent bedroom, the double bed takes up most of the space. In the long night that follows, I become aware of something new. Of the growling, hungry animal inside me that I never knew existed. Where did it come from? Is it just the skill of the courtesan, trained to extract the best from her clients? My father certainly would have disapproved. Never mind all those bogus claims of a red-hot love life. When it came to it, he had been rather prissy on the subject: even though the air had been thick with it at times, with all those Satellites clustered around him breathing a pious and sexual reverence, and he the high priest of the cult robed so chastely.

As for me, I know I can stay in this bed the rest of my life, submerged in the recondite and sensuous pleasures of a world hitherto so alien. Yet there is enough of my father in me—rational and mathematical, aware of the beauty though cool enough to remain emotionally uninvested—to recognize the great danger I am in: the danger that faces any addict. The more I stay, the less I want from the outside world.

This is enough, my senses cry out. *I want nothing more.*

Fool! says my mind. *Are you crazy? There's a whole world out there for you to conquer.*

*

Janine shook me awake. 'Aren't you late?'

Scrambling into my clothes, I sprinted for the bus, squeaking in at ten to eight to find them all waiting outside. They had never seen me in decent attire before, so I was naturally the butt this morning of all the jokes, the Posh Paki jokes.

I opened the door to let them in.

'Where's the ladder?' asked Sean.

The two-stage ladder that was lying along the stairs was gone.

'Bastards! They knew you weren't in last night.'

But how did they get in? There was no sign of a break-in. The thought of Mr Brown driving all the way from Guildford to lift a ladder was too absurd to contemplate. A little later, Jo called out from the basement. We all trooped down. What I saw made my blood run cold. In the corner was a large human turd. By its side, the pickaxe. The thief had been down there, armed with the pickaxe, while I was showing Douglas around. After Douglas left, I was there for ten more minutes. Had I gone down to the cellar for my usual bucket of water I would not be alive now. The cellar was barely six feet high and six feet wide. You could do a lot of damage with a pickaxe in that confined space, and there would have been no escape.

'Shall we call the police?' I asked.

They all laughed. This was Brixton in 1980. 'When we lost the drill from Sandmere, we called in the fuzz,' Sean explained. 'Half an hour later, a bobby on a bike pedalled up. He wheeled the bike inside the house. The first thing he asked was, "Is my bike safe in this corridor?"'

*

Douglas began work and I watched fascinated. He wielded his trowel like a tennis player with a particularly elegant backhand. It was like watching Wimbledon from the royal box. The rear room leading out to the garden needed to be plastered entirely, which made my decorating easy because no woodchip would be needed then, only paint. I just had to wait till the plaster dried and turned colour, from an earthy brown to the palest mushroom pink. I spent the afternoon at the hire shop, settling up for the stolen ladder from the security deposit. We decided not to hire another till the actual day the downpipes were to be replaced, to minimize losses.

'A watcher, that's what you need,' Sean winked. 'If you're going to be spending any more nights away.'

'You have anyone in mind?'

He shook his head.

When we got back from the hire shop there was a man in the front yard, in an anorak almost as shiny as mine, glasses and cloth cap.

'I'm Malachy,' he said mournfully, 'the Drains Inspector.'

I felt Sean go rigid by my side.

'Have you tested the drains? I think we need to do a little test, don't you?'

Half an hour later the manhole covers were up, and the drains plugs—like small chunky frisbees, fetched in haste from Sandmere—screwed in firmly at either end. The entire system was then filled with water to see if there were leaks. Sean and I watched in dismay as the water levels sank rapidly.

'I think you'll need to replace the entire drainage system, don't you?'

'Oh shit,' I said.

'Yes,' agreed Mr Malachy laconically. 'Shit.'

I was stretched to the limit as it was. Now another big expense. I would have to start digging: all the way from the back garden, underneath the floorboards of the back addition, through the cellar and out to the road. I had no idea then that this job, digging drains, would be the most physically arduous task I would ever undertake in my life, bestowing—as a sort of reward or miraculous side effect—the most articulated and defined back muscles a man could ever hope to have.

*

A priest with a rum-rich voice and Portuguese name intoned the prayers. Then he led the congregation in the hymns. It was touching to hear the Satellites singing—in their querulous, quavering voices—even the ones who were not Christian. They were, after all, sworn members of that other deeper, more fundamental faith, the Worship of the Blessed Louis.

I planted a kiss on that marble-cold forehead and the men from Raymond's closed the coffin lid. Afterwards, another short homily at the crematorium, very short because there was a queue: only one oven was working and there were many parties of people waiting patiently for their own particular death. The Satellites had pulled strings so we could jump the queue.

'Press the green button, Big Feller,' they whispered in my ear, as if I might press some other button by mistake, consigning him to another more esoteric heaven.

Back home Myrna opened up the corrugated cardboard boxes lined with newspaper, containing the patties, cutlets and pancake rolls. The crowd—mostly unidentified strangers—fell on them. Nothing sharpens the appetite like a good funeral. Though as funerals went, this one had not been that good. No politicians in white sarongs, no lawyers in dandruffed black coats shiny with grease and rapaciousness, no boy scouts, no plump white actress wiping away a practised tear from a mascaraed eye. My father had not known anyone prominent or rich; he had not cared to. Indeed, he had considered it the height of vulgarity for people to advertise their qualifications or flaunt their wealth—the way they did in modern Sri Lanka where the rich would tattoo the very dollars to their forehead if they possibly could.

'For this coming week we have organized a rota of people to sleep in the house with you, Big Feller,' the Satellites said. 'We're taking turns. It's not good for you to sleep alone in a funeral house.'

'Alone?' I pointed silently at the various faux-relations bedding down for the night in odd corners, sad no doubt that there was no liquor in the house to prolong the party. After much bickering the Satellites were persuaded to go home.

I went in and closed the door to my room. Grief must be faced squarely and alone: a man in a walled garden, watching the sun set. A thin line of uncertain wavering brilliance at the top of the mellow brickwork, there for one brief moment then gone, leaving behind only the blank page of an unreadable sky. The insignificant noises outside my room faded away as I sat in silence; and wave after wave of grief washed over me, thin and clear and bright like breakers on an early morning shore. His absence was so palpable, so tactile that I could reach out all around and touch it. I had hated and despised him for so much of my life; I had spent the last years barely talking to him; there had been no great rapprochement during his last days, as there is in films. He and I had been too busy fighting the bureaucracy of death—barely surviving from day to day, keeping our heads above water—to think of any nobler objective.

And now he was gone. I could not even reach out for the familiar comforts of hate or indifference any more. All I had was this silence.

Then, somewhere in the watches of that sleepless night, it came to me: that grief is only the transmutation of love, of the very same chemical composition—liquid, undistilled—the one inevitably turning to the other like ice to water. It had taken the half-completed life and early death of one man for me to discover this truth.

14

She buzzed me up, opening the door in her mink coat and high heels. And nothing else.

'Fur coat, no knickers,' she said apologetically. Then she burst out laughing, raucous and uncontrolled.

Once she had quietened down, I told her about the break-in. 'You don't by any chance know anyone who could be a watcher on the site, do you?'

She thought a bit. 'I don't think so, but I'll keep it in mind.'

Friendly but unsympathetic: the way a man would be with another man's woes. How I could have done with my army of Satellites just then, standing guard over me, standing guard over my life!

As if she could read my thoughts, Janine said, 'You know, I had the strangest phone call last week? From my sister-in-law. Ex-sister-in-law.'

I must have looked puzzled because she went on to explain. 'Myrna, I mean.'

'Myrna?'

'I know. She hasn't spoken to me in, what, ten years?'

'And?'

'A long rambling call. The crux of it is—she wants to come on holiday. Asked if she could stay here.' She looked closely at me. 'This hasn't anything to do with you, has it?'

Cunning Myrna! What better way to spy on us? My father would have approved of this sharp move.

'So what did you say?'

'What could I say? I said yes, of course she must come and stay. Best to keep an old cow like her happy. You never know what she might be capable of if she took against me.'

'You didn't! What about us?'

She looked at me mischievously. 'We'll have to think of other ways to outwit her, won't we? Not too difficult, I promise. Wasn't always the brightest bulb in the chandelier, our Myrna.'

An interesting choice of phrase, one my father had used all the time. I thought with a sudden spurt of jealousy: how well had she known him?

Then we went into the bedroom and shut the door on the world. All else was forgotten: Myrna's plots and my work deadlines and ghosts who stole ladders. For one brief moment I think I even forgot about my father.

*

I let the guys into the house next morning and there seemed to be no break-in. Nothing taken. Then Sean let out a yelp from the kitchen. The entire white work surface was covered in turmeric.

'You'll never get the stains off! That's vindictive, that is.'

Who could have done this, with nothing whatsoever to gain from it? 'Guys,' I said desperately. 'I need a watcher. Any volunteers?'

'You'll have to stay in yourself, won't you? Watch over the house. Less of the mistress, ha!'

The workers had barely left when Janak arrived, waving an airmail letter in my face. He was alone.

'Do you think one of your illegals might like to moonlight as a watcher on this site?' I asked.

He shook his head. 'Not a chance. They're on shift work, so they won't be able to turn up regularly. Besides, if something goes really wrong and the police have to be called, they'll be put on the next boat back to Sri Lanka. They can't take the risk. Anyway, never mind all that, we have a bigger problem on our hands.'

He began to read from the letter:

Darling Janak,

Our Big Feller has been compromised! Yes, can you believe it? Your Aunt (I hesitate to call her that, you know the runaround she gave your poor Uncle Ivor, how he never recovered?) has got her clutches into him. I hear he has even moved in with her.

Yes, can you believe it? Poor, poor, Louis. I don't know what he did to deserve this. And after his death too! Anyway, drastic events call for drastic measures. I have booked myself on UL504 arriving November 25. Don't tell me. I'll freeze to death in that godforsaken country, I know. But I am doing this for Louis. I know he'll never forgive me if I don't. Even if he's dead.

I have asked to stay with that brazen hussy and she has readily agreed. (There is something very suspicious about that. I wonder what she is plotting. Do you think she will try to poison me?) But hopefully my presence will put a stop to their shenanigans. I will sacrifice myself, even if it kills me. I am quite looking forward to seeing you too. Please write and tell me what you might want in the way of chutneys, pickles and jams.

In haste,

Your loving mother.

'I don't see why *you* can't put her up. She's your mother after all.'

'Me?' He looked scandalized. 'What would I do with George?'

'Drop him home to Mummy. I'm sure he has homework.'

'Ha, very funny. What about you? Does Janine remember to change your nappies?'

'Enough. We have to cover for each other. Janine's more than a match for Myrna. Let her stay there.'

'My mother thinks of you as her son. Don't let her down.'

There we were, two grown men, surviving in what was probably the toughest inner-city district of London, worried sick about what our mothers back home might think. It was absurd how much this mattered to us, to what great pains we were prepared to go to hide facts. I learnt later that half the Sri Lankan population of London was doing the same, changing their personae, chameleon-like, for the two weeks of every year that they went back home, reverting to their normal adult lives the moment the plane touched down at Heathrow. A fact that would be laughable if it weren't so tragic.

*

That night I remained at home, barricading myself into the topmost room of the house with a length of old iron gas pipe. All night I could hear them scrabbling about downstairs. At one point, I thought I heard heavy breathing outside my door. By morning my nerves were in shreds.

The Mulrooneys were expected. They never arrived till mid-morning, and while the rest of us nourished ourselves at the caff feasting on animal fats, the Mulrooneys dined lightly off Tupperware in secluded corners of the house, nibbling on slivers of elegant carrot and cauliflower.

'You don't by any chance know of someone who could be a watcher here on the site?' I asked desperately.

The Mulrooneys paused mid-carrot and gave each other significant looks. 'I think so, yes,' they said in a slightly superior tone.

*

This is how Michael came into the story, arriving at seven that evening, already swaying after a pint or two. But beggars can't be choosers so I hired him on the spot.

'You can kip down in the front room. If you come by eight every evening it's enough.'

With Michael in the house I began getting a good night's sleep. In some strange way I felt obliged to stay behind to keep him company, so it was easier to resist the corrosive pleasures of the Pink Palace. I decided to ration myself to weekends and one day mid-week: a decision that made me feel in control of this addiction. Janine did not seem to mind. When I was there, she was happy. When I said I could not make it, she was philosophical. I realized that it was this equanimity that made her so desirable.

'So you have a watcher now?'

'A friend of the Mulrooneys. Michael.'

'Michael?'

'Why? Do you know him?'

'I don't think so.'

The nights I slept at Tintern I told Michael he need not come in till ten. He rolled in promptly at that hour, swaying dangerously. He would look at me fiercely, muttering in fluent Gaelic. Being fair-minded, he slipped into English every once in a while for my benefit, so I could get a hint of what he was saying.

'Black bastard!' he growled, louring over me, peering minutely at my face the way drunks do. 'You *dirty* black bastard.'

I didn't mind, really I didn't. I'm all for proficiency in the dead languages.

Then he crashed to the ground like a felled coconut tree. Moments later, the rich vibrato of his snoring began, rising through the floorboards with the warmth and resonance of an orchestra, loud enough to scare away any ghost.

On the rare occasion he was sober, we talked. The first thing I realized was how much he loathed the Mulrooneys.

'Shower of bastards! Think they're English, do they? Just because they lived here a couple of years. Ha!'

'What's wrong with that?'

'Well, they're Irish, aren't they? Every bit Irish as I am. They speak Gaelic better than I do. Just pretending they've forgotten.'

Janak had told me the story of a Sri Lankan friend of his who, within a week of arriving in London, had forgotten his Sinhalese, miraculously acquiring a cardboard English accent. I realized that we immigrants had more in common with each other than we knew.

'Then they got themselves this job at the Palace. Changing the plug on the toaster or something.' He snickered. 'So now they're all lords.'

'How do you know them?'

He looked at me pityingly. 'They're my brothers, aren't they?'

*

Just when I thought it could not get any colder the temperature dropped another couple of degrees. I was out in the backyard now, digging a channel from manhole to manhole for the new drainage system. Jo had taught me how to manoeuvre the water-logged London clay—heavy as pig iron—on to the tip of the shovel, flinging it over my shoulder with a turn of the wrist. It was all in the timing of the movement, the skill of your leverage. But before you could get to the clay, there were ten inches of concrete to break: the result, no doubt, of many happy Sundays spent by Mr Brown concreting his backyard. After a day my hands were red and raw. Then the calluses formed and became as hard and leathery as the scales of an alligator. You began the morning in four layers of clothing. Within an hour, you would strip to the waist. But if you stopped work for even ten minutes the cold would come back, searing and ferocious, as if your chest were being branded all over by frozen irons.

Every time I stopped I looked up at the sky, luminous and grey as pearls, and ineffably sad. I had left behind in Sri Lanka a well of grief caused by the death of my father, the depths of which I had not fully plumbed. Yet all the while the skies overhead had smiled and smiled with foolish unreasonable happiness. Here it was absolutely the reverse: I worked all day with the joyous warm glow of physical hardship. Yet all around whenever I stopped was emptiness, the echo of silence: as if the very world were mourning the death of its soul. The skies seemed to say: *Laugh all you want, enjoy yourself. You will come to understand soon enough, as we have done, the void that underpins your existence.*

The misery, like so much else in the West, had been conveniently outsourced; but the truth—the only truth you need know—was that winter would return. For a tropical islander this was the essential Faustian pact, the price he had so willingly paid to come here: one he would never be able to recoup however long he might live in the country.

I was glad then of that other pact, the one I had made with myself. That however much I enjoyed myself, however much money I made or did not make, I would return home when I was thirty.

Years later it was discovered that a lack of light did something to the chemistry of people's brains, altering their sensibilities. We who came from light-filled worlds were long aware of this, even if there were no scientific proofs back then to pin our convictions on.

15

I remember the day of the almsgiving after my father's death as one of the most beautiful I have ever seen. Perhaps every day had been like that; but my father and I had spent the last half year with our heads down—two marathon runners afraid to look up, fearing the inevitability of the finish line, concentrating instead on the minute bumps and flaws of the track. We knew our job was merely to stay the course, reach the end. It was an entirely democratic race, free and fair: nobody won, all winners were losers. What awaited you at the conclusion was annihilation, nothingness, the zero in the equation.

Now the end had come and gone, and I raised my head, and the ravishing full blue of the tropic sky enveloped me in its folds as soft as a baby's blanket. A couple of days before the almsgiving, as if by silent arrangement, I woke up to find the Satellites cleaning the house.

'Pass the Vim,' they said to each other in the same tones as 'pass the salt'. As a cabal they had always had their differences—as any cabinet of ministers must—so it was heart-warming to see this government acting so concertedly, in unison, especially when the head of state had long since departed. I knew that it was the first and last time Clifford Road would attain such a shine. When I offered to help they were horrified.

'Sit down, Big Feller, relax. You've had such a time of it. Save your energy for the crowds.'

And crowds there were. Myrna had cooked to feed an army: an army that marched on its stomach, capriciously laying waste to the country through which it marched.

'So, what will you do with yourself, Sanjay?' they asked.

What was I meant to do with myself? It was my father who had died. Was I meant to roll my eyeballs and shiver as if possessed, losing the only bit of self-control I'd ever had? I realized that some major reshuffle was expected of me. Only I did not know what.

'Of course, you will now think of going *abroad*,' one old matron told me firmly. Abroad was that great white shark swimming out there: the dream of every sensible Sri Lankan was to be swallowed by it. Once that narrative had been so definitively inserted into my head I found myself expanding on it, embellishing it with rhinestones and fake diamonds, giving it a shiny, synthetic personality all of its own.

So it was no surprise when I heard myself say quite loudly, 'Oh, you know, I think I'd quite like to visit

Italy? I always wanted to see Siena, Montepulciano, Anghiari . . . My father too, only he never quite made it.'

Nobody there had ever been to Italy. My father's friends, even his enemies, all of whom were there that day (the seventh-day almsgiving is almost obligatory for enemies), were not the sort of people who went to Italy on holiday. Yala and Habarana were more their beat. So I said Italy to shut them up. And it did.

*

'You have two more weeks,' Janine reminded me. 'When do you want me to market the flats?'

I had progressed from the outside to the back addition room where Jo had removed the floorboards and cut some joists so that I could dig my way through to the cellar. If any prospective punters came now, they would run a mile, so the time was not yet right; but it was only a matter of a day to put the flooring back and re-touch the paintwork once the new drains were laid.

I never failed to marvel at how Janine could hold both business and pleasure aspects of our relationship in her head simultaneously. As for me, all thoughts of business were erased from my head the moment I entered the Pink Palace. I would rush there straight from work. At the door she would make me strip so the mud of my jeans would not soil her flat. Or so she said. I think it gave her a sense of power to have a naked man at her table, dining on boeuf bourguignon. Nudity left her entirely unfazed. She was a good twenty years older than me, at an age when you might think she would be insecure about her appearance before a much younger man; but not at all.

'I'm sorry about my wobbly bits,' she would say, slapping whichever part of her was in question, but she was not sorry at all. Ageing to her was part of the natural biological process. If you did not like it, if it made you uncomfortable, you could go elsewhere. All this—the sense of control she exuded—only drew me in tighter. I was the novice, the ingénue wandering open-mouthed and visa-free through this other country—where normal laws did not seem to pertain.

The joy that resulted was a different fish to that other happiness of the building site. Together with your clothes you surrendered reason at the door, like a drunk coming home at night, feeling his way to the light switch with his eyes closed. This was purely a journey of the heart—negotiated by the coordinates of touch and smell and taste alone. There was no possession by the mind of those empty spaces as in that other happiness. Here, you were blind as well as naked, divested of all rationality. When I think back all these years later, there is so little of the Pink Palace that I remember—its physical appearance, its volumes. The memory is all in the fingers. I am the blind pianist whose fingers involuntarily twitch when the first chords of the concerto begin to play.

Being a novice I was unaware too of that other narrative that Sri Lankan society espoused: that of the brazen older woman ensnaring and bewitching the younger man, ruining him in a way that left him unfit ever afterwards to live a normal life, with a partner his own age. The London of 1980 was not that much different. It was perfectly acceptable, even admired, for an older man to bed a woman young enough to be his daughter. But a woman even two years older than her man? Horror of horrors! Back then there were no French presidents to blaze a trail. Only the story of the spider weaving her web to entrap the innocent fly. Nobody spared a thought for the fly—all too willing, all too often an absolutely delighted victim.

You must remember that I had never had sex before; now I was thrown into the deep end. My experience of women till now had been the cabal—a chocolate box selection of the softest, most sweet-hearted women you could ever hope to meet, all of them experienced in the art of pandering to one monster of a man. The word 'pander' did not enter Janine's vocabulary. You either had sex or you didn't. You were either satisfied or you weren't. There was no agonizing either way. 'I have my needs,' she stated simply. *I have my needs*. For a Sri Lankan woman this was nothing short of unique.

'I have as little to do with Sri Lankans as I can,' she said. 'Sri Lankans are like wine, they don't travel well. When I see how England affects them—their pathetic efforts at becoming "civilized", which of course come down at the end of the day to that suburban bungalow in Surbiton . . .' she shook her head in horror.

Nobody could have accused her of compromise. She had lived in England these past twenty years.

Yet nothing of England had rubbed off on her. I could see how Myrna and the others might find her impossibly coarse, too rough and ready for their 'refined' middle class sensibilities. Meeting her for the first time was like having a glass of iced water thrown in your face.

So I waited with dread for the forthcoming confrontation between the ex-sisters-in-law.

'Let's enjoy ourselves while we can,' Janine said, as if she were some sort of witch who could read my mind. 'It'll all come to a dead stop when the old cow arrives.'

'Why? You can come to Tintern,' I suggested.

'What? With your watcher there? To become the laughing stock of your workers?'

'I thought that sort of thing didn't bother you?'

She laughed.

'In that case, I'll have to give him a holiday.'

'You do that and I'll think about it.'

*

There was an evangelical church at the end of Tintern Street. All Saturday the road was filled with West Indians going to prayer, in patent leather court shoes and exuberant hats with bunches of grapes on them. There was much clapping and singing, and the flourish of tambourines. There is no one so cynical as a building worker, yet even in our hardened state we could not fail to be uplifted by this joyful uproar.

Sunday by contrast was lonely and quiet. There were no workers and I was left alone to my drains and my thoughts. Consciously or not, I ran and re-ran in my head the events of the past year. The truths that emerged from this replaying seemed more solid somehow, scored as they were with the clearer outlines of hindsight.

By three in the afternoon it was dark in that back room. I worked with the aid of an extension lamp. It was colder inside the house than out, with a dampness that cut through to your bones. I piled the black waterlogged earth on either side of me as I dug into the trench, like banks on either side of a road. It was so cold I could no longer feel my hands even though I kept on swinging the pick into the frozen ground.

You know how it is when a sudden silence descends on you, muffling the silence that is already there? As if someone is standing silently at the door, blocking the light and air into the room? I looked up into the darkness beyond my lamp. There was nobody there.

Suddenly, I felt this thing settle on me, as if the earth itself had come to life and was pressing down, soft and damp and unyielding, stifling me with a pillow to my face. I found I could not breathe. I knew then that I was in the presence of death: unrequited, unforgiving; unceasingly famished.

Haven't you had enough from me? I wanted to shout. *Leave me alone!* But my mouth was full and I was choking, and it was easier to yield without struggle, to remain silent. And as I surrendered I felt immeasurably, inconsolably sad—at the emptiness of this world, and even more at the emptiness that must lie beyond. I don't know how long I stayed like this, motionless, before managing to struggle out of the trench.

Who knew how many deaths had taken place in this old house during its long history? Outside the house it was warmer, there was a powdery rain falling. Janak would not be back from work yet and I was too ashamed to take refuge in Janine's office. Instead, I tramped up and down those bleak desolate streets for the next hour, too afraid to go back into the house. Finally I stepped into Bilquis's shop, into the comforting mildewed warmth of her canned goods.

'What's the matter, love? You seen a ghost or something?'

'Nah, just feeling a little cold, that's all.'

There was something about her unfailing good cheer that brought the colour back to my face. I left for Janine's as soon as I knew she'd be home. I could not go back into the house again that night. Let Michael deal with whatever was inside.

16

Christmas was coming and Bilquis had already strung up a row of Santas, flashing red green and purple along her front window.

'Christmas is for everyone, not just for Christmas,' she explained, paraphrasing a favourite car sticker of the time. On site the Mulrooneys talked of nothing but their forthcoming Christmas dinner.

'Nice bit of goose is what I fancy,' said Pat Mulrooney. 'Traditional English fare.'

I could almost hear Michael going 'hah!' in the background.

Since none of us was invited to this epic feast, it was academic whether they had goose or turkey; or even masala vadais.

'Is Michael joining you?'

'You joking? The wives wouldn't stand for it. He'd only get drunk and insult the Queen.'

'Michael's a loner,' Ted explained kindly. 'Much happier on his own.'

'Is he married?'

'Was. A while back. To a darki—I mean a coloured woman.'

'Educated too, from what I remember,' Pat said. 'Much too good for him.'

As for the rest of us, we were in quite a state with our impending Sri Lankan arrival.

'I'm putting you in charge,' Janak said, eyeing me sternly. 'She's only coming to sort *you* out, so you're responsible, right?'

'And George?'

He looked pained. 'The thing is, George refuses to disappear. I've begged and begged. "I want to meet my *mother-in-law*," he says. So I can't risk having Myrna in the house. I have to tell her it's overflowing with tenants. Which is true anyway. And that means,' he fixed me with his stern look again, 'all the entertainment will be done here at Tintern, you understand? This will be base camp.'

'Gee thanks,' I said.

'It's the least you can do. Having got us into all this trouble.'

*

I had progressed to the cellar now, the scene of my possible demise had the burglar had his way. At least it was warmer down there. My trainers, which had holes in them, were wet and my socks soaking.

There was a sudden flash and the cellar filled with smoke. I found myself thrown five feet back, miraculously still on my feet. Even more miraculously, I was still alive. The pick had struck a live power cable—the mains supply into the house. The handle of the pick was wooden. That was what had saved me.

'Somebody really doesn't like you,' was Sean's comment. He was a superstitious soul and no one took him seriously. As for me, I felt light-headed, cavalier, having cheated death yet again. Really, it seemed to me, I was unkillable that month of November.

Back home, had the Satellites had their way—though my father would probably have never allowed it—they would have organized a lime-cutting ceremony to ward off the malign influences I was obviously under. Here I had to make do with a stiff drink.

Janak and George met me at The Swan. 'Sell the bottom flat as well,' they said. 'Move on. Something in the house seems to disagree with you.'

'Tell me about my mother-in-law,' George said cozily. 'I want to know *all* about her.'

Janak shot me a sick look over the top of his head.

'She's the best cook in the world. The mother I never had.'

'Can't *wait* to meet her!'

Janak stuck two fingers down his throat and made silent vomiting motions.

'Just imagine,' I said. 'If I get together with Janine, you two will be my nephews!'

'Never mind nephews. When are you going to meet your cousins?'

'Cousins?'

'The ones in Devon or wherever?'

I got up from the table. 'My round. Who's having what? I need to get drunk tonight. To celebrate my second near-death experience of the month. Here's to many more!'

*

In the confines of Janine's pretty pink safe house, I could not help but marvel at how lucky I was: to have the option of a clean well-lit existence at night, running parallel to the daytime realities of those dark Brixton streets. I was aware too of how weak I was: of my inability to switch languages with any ease. The more I relied on her night-time comforts the more they seemed to sap my stamina for survival in the daytime world. Conversely, after half an hour back on site—once I had dug myself into a hole inside that damp cellar—I was as happy as a child at the beach, digging away with his bucket and spade. The day only appeared dismal and dingy and untenable when viewed from within the brilliance of the night.

Perhaps this would be the story of the rest of my life. Perhaps I was condemned to spending it see-sawing between the two—the sex-saturated gluttony of the one, and the monk-like, sweat-ridden existence of the other.

But that night Janine sat up in bed and said: 'Right. I want you out of here in the morning.' Almost as if she were conspiring with the fates to teach me a lesson: that I should take no pleasure for granted.

'But Myrna doesn't arrive for another couple of days.'

'Never mind. I need to psych myself up. She's my sister-in-law.'

'Ex.'

'In Sri Lanka your relations never leave you. However much you may want them to. A marriage is for life, not just for Christmas.'

'You're beginning to sound like Bilquis.'

'Who's Bilquis? Some fuckbuddy of yours?'

Next morning I left with my toothbrush, my only belonging in her house.

'Remember,' she said, 'she'll bring me for sure to visit you at the site, so she can observe us, see how we react to each other. Don't let me down. You don't know me, right?'

'As if I ever did,' I mumbled. But I don't think she heard.

*

I went to work feeling abandoned, bereft. I felt more sad to see that it did not seem to matter to her one way or the other, this sex-free fortnight. (I did not actually know how long Myrna was planning to stay. I reckoned she would not be able to stay away longer than a couple of weeks.)

As if to underline the professionalism henceforth of our relationship, a signboard went up outside the house that morning, nailed to the parapet wall: *For Sale.*

Richard Woking Estates. I still did not have a phone on site; she would bring clients whenever she wanted, no need of an appointment.

'But we're strangers, okay?'

'Of course. Why would you know some random Asian labourer on a building site?' If there was any bitterness in my voice she did not seem to hear it.

Mid-morning, I heard the familiar clip-clop of shoes on the floorboards directly overhead, the swishy-swish of her skirt, and my fingers involuntarily trembled with the physical memory of those thighs encased in that artificial material. I did not see who it was she had brought. They left after ten minutes.

Michael came in that evening with a one-and-a-half litre brown bottle of Liebfraumilch, the drink of choice those days of the discerning builder. We shared it, me seated on the hedgehog, him on the floor. As the level in the bottle dipped, he got more maudlin.

'You know I wasn't always like this?'

'I'm sure,' I agreed politely.

'Had a decent job. Wife too; though *she* wasn't decent,' he sniggered. 'Lucky old me!'

'So what happened?'

'The bottle happened, innit? Lost the job, everything. Wife kicked me out.' He took a swig of wine. 'Said she'd have me back the day I cleaned up. Don't know though. Having far too good a time she is. Always was a good time girl.'

'Mine kicked me out too. And your brothers? '

He began swearing in Gaelic. 'Bastards!' he said finally, switching languages for my benefit. 'Jumped-up bunch of bloody bastards—'

'Tell me,' I said, interrupting this diatribe. 'You sleep okay at night? Noises disturb you or anything?'

'Noises? What noises? Even World War III wouldn't wake me up!'

'Comforting to know,' I replied.

*

Tonight I really cannot sleep. Perhaps it is the wine, sweet as lemonade, sulphite-ridden, laced with preservatives. Perhaps it is because I am sleeping in my own bed after so long, devoid of company. *What is she doing now? Why did she want to get rid of me so early? Who is she entertaining? Most important of all, is she missing me as much as I am missing her?* I think I know the answer to that one. It isn't the answer I want to face up to.

Somewhere in the early hours of the morning, when I do not really know whether I am awake or asleep—when reality and dream are so tightly fused that they are actually the same—the noises begin. It is almost a relief. I am the theatre-goer at the start of a much-delayed performance, waiting for the curtain to go up, aware of vague shapes and sounds issuing from behind the cloth. Suddenly, noiselessly, the drapery has risen and I find I am actually in the play, in that dreamland which is also a nightmare; a nightmare that you know in your sad heart it is your lot to live through. There is no way around.

Through it all I hear the counterpoint of Michael's snores, comforting as drum rolls from the orchestra pit. I can hear laughter and talk, the audience hasn't settled down yet. Suddenly, something makes me sit up in bed. Someone is humming off-key the theme to the BBC World Service, the Lilliburlero, a tune I grew up with, familiar and inevitable.

I get out of bed. I walk the few steps down to the kitchen, and there he is, hunched over his favourite transistor radio at the kitchen table. Only there is no radio.

He stops humming and looks up when he hears me at the door. 'Good evening, Big Feller,' my father says.

17

You know it is your father, so no harm can come to you. Still, you are petrified. *Who or what is this? Is it a ghost? Is it for real?*

'Don't be alarmed,' he says. 'I'm only here because you wanted me here.'

This matter-of-fact smugness only makes me angry; my fear is forgotten. This thing—whatever you like to call it—may not be for real, but it sure as hell reminds me of the old man.

'You're here for me?' I shout. 'Are you out of your mind? Get the fuck out! Leave me alone. You've ruined my life enough!'

'Shh,' he says. 'You'll wake up the staff.'

'Staff? *Staff?*'

'Calm down, you're overwrought. This funeral thing has really done you in.'

'Whose fault is that?'

'Don't shout. Remember only you can hear me, but we can all hear *you*. They'll have you locked up for talking to yourself.'

'Get out!'

He throws up his haunted hands in that theatrical gesture I know so well. 'I decide out of the goodness of my heart to come over and give you a helping hand. This is all the thanks I get.'

'Oh, fuck off!'

'Sanjay, Sanjay,' he says reprovingly. 'You're not yourself. Go back to sleep, we'll talk in the morning.'

'You wish!' I shout. Then I realize he is no longer there.

*

So who is the madman here? Did I imagine all this? Have I, in some Joan of Arc way, conjured him up to fulfil some mental need of mine? Who or what exactly is this misbegotten metaphysical monster? It certainly sounds like my father. It has his cussed ways about it and his quarrelsome nature. Abandoning all spectral speculation I go back to bed. For the first time ever in this house, I sink into a sleep so deep that the next thing I know, the workers are banging on the door to be let in.

'You look a wreck,' Sean says with a wink. 'These early nights are killing you.'

I shake my head and drink up my PG Tips greedily, praying my father doesn't appear. *It was a dream*, I decide, *brewed up by bad wine*.

I am nearly done with the drains. I go with Sean to a huge builders' yard on Wandsworth Road to buy six foot-lengths of clay drain pipe, the black plastic collars, the glazed semi-engineering bricks for the manholes and the monstrous terracotta end piece called an interceptor, through which you can push your shit (should you need to) out into the main sewer under the road. At the end of all this I will be an authority on drains, an expert shit-shooter, a veritable Doctor of Turds.

Throughout the day, Janine drops in at least twice with prospective clients. I hear but don't see her. So near, yet so far. How does she handle this separation so coolly? She must have plenty of experience, this Queen of Tarts. Meanwhile I am stuck in my hole digging, these disloyal thoughts swirling around my head like sewage in a manhole.

By evening I was beginning to doubt if I had even seen my father the previous night. Could it be that I had hallucinated? I finally came to the conclusion that it must have been some sort of dream within a dream, not to be taken seriously. Michael staggered in for duty, falling with a crash to the floor of the downstairs front room. I was continually amazed at how he always rose next morning, pink-cheeked and seemingly unscathed by these dramatic falls. Perhaps there were so many dents in him already that any new ones went unnoticed. I left him snuffling and mumbling on the floor, going upstairs to the kitchen to fix myself my nightly cheese sandwich. No sign of any ghosts. Heaving a sigh of relief I went up to bed. I had just brushed my teeth and tucked myself in when my father appeared. Seated at the foot of the bed.

'Thought I'd leave you alone during the day,' he explained. 'Can't have you shouting to yourself, can we? What would the workers say?'

'You're harassing me, you know that? Why are you doing this to me?'

'I'm here to protect you.'

'Protect me? Hah! The only thing I need is protection *from* you.'

'You think this is easy for me? Turning up at will? I have to work *very hard* to manifest myself.'

'Manifest? Hard? You never worked hard in your life. You're dead. Try to remember that. We're barely finished with the funeral.'

'Ah yes, that funeral. I need to speak to you about it, Big Feller.' He wrinkled his nose. 'A bit of a shabby affair, wasn't it? And oh good God, the food . . . !'

'Why? What was wrong with the food?'

'That Myrna? Hopeless . . .'

'If you want to complain, tell her yourself. She's coming in two days.'

My father began to shake his head. 'That's it, you see. All communication has to be through you. I can't manifest myself to just anyone. Only the next of kin.'

'Well, you're not using me as some sort of postbox,' I shouted. 'What's it matter anyway? You're dead. *Cremated*. You went up in a cloud of smoke. *Pff!* Just like that!'

'Just like that,' he agreed sadly. 'I know.' We sat there for a while not saying anything to each other. It was quite like old times.

Then he said a little absently, 'Smoking kills,' and vanished.

I felt sorry then. It's not good manners to be nasty to ghosts. They have feelings too.

'You were shouting a lot last night,' Michael informed me the next morning. 'I nearly came up to see what the matter was.'

'I always shout in my sleep,' I explained. 'It's something I like to do.'

*

That afternoon I finished the digging. I could hardly believe it. Sean laid the drain pipes end to end, joining each one to the next with a well-lubricated plastic collar, the entire system running from the backyard to the very front of the cellar, with the gentlest drop of one in forty: all his laying completed in one swift hour, as opposed to my one week of hard digging. I mixed up a couple of buckets of concrete to bed the collars, the pipes themselves lying loose in the earth so there would be a certain amount of give to the whole system. Tomorrow, after the concrete had set, Sean would build the brick manholes at either end.

We were just sitting down to our tea when the bell rang. Mr Malachy stood forlornly outside. 'I'll come in if I may?'

Douglas had been plastering all day. The front corridor was full of smoke. Mr Malachy's nose quivered like a rabbit's. 'Delicious,' he said sorrowfully.

'Herbal,' I explained. 'Sri Lankan remedy. Ayurveda.'

In fact the whole site was floating. Mr Malachy just stood there, taking in the air.

'Do you want some tea?' I asked quickly before any lift-off could take place.

He followed me silently into the kitchen, casting a pall over our teatime conversation, his presence like thunder at a picnic. 'We're not ready for you yet,' I said, making a vain effort at inconsequential teatime chatter. 'We'll be ready the day after. Perhaps you could come back then?'

Mr Malachy began to giggle. 'I don't know what it is about this site,' he said, leaning forward confidentially. 'I just don't feel like getting up when I sit down, you know?'

'Yeah, man,' said Douglas appreciatively. '*Right on!*'

We sat in silence for another little while, the workers fidgeting like kids at Sunday school. I rather wished my father had appeared just then, dripping ectoplasm all over the tea things to make Mr Malachy run shrieking into the night. No such luck. Ghosts. Never there when you need them. All over you when you don't.

Finally I got up. 'We're closing up for the night,' I told Mr Malachy. 'We'll see you day after, shall we?' I walked him out. He turned round one more time and giggled, as I shut the door politely in his face.

*

I'd had all day to think about what my father had said. *Protection? From whom? And why go to all that trouble to 'manifest' himself before me?* My father, always the laziest man alive, so admirably hyperactive in death. It did not make sense at all. I found myself looking forward to his next appearance. It happened very late.

'Sorry, got held up in traffic.'

'Traffic?'

'Yes. The others.'

'Tell me,' I said a little combatively. 'Protection. You're joking, right? You always were the biggest bullshitter in town.'

'Of course. The turmeric in the kitchen, the axe in the basement, the live cable. All bullshit, I suppose.'

'There's a perfectly rational explanation! Thieves are getting into the house.'

He bowed his head gracefully. 'If you say so, Sanjay, if you say so. Now, never mind all that. Tell me about this old woman you're shacked up with.'

'Old? She's younger than you!'

'Isn't it kind of a faggy thing to do?'

'Faggy? *Faggy*? Oh fuck off, you paranormal prick!'

'Language, Sanjay, language.'

'There's only Michael downstairs. He could teach you a thing or two about swearing.'

'Why do you keep him on? I'm here now, Big Feller, for anything. Ask and you shall receive.'

Ask? I was silent for a long while. There was so much to ask, where even to begin? But something about that frozen cold space made my mind fizz, fermenting what little courage I had into this great gaseous cloud of bravado. 'Actually there's one thing,' I said finally. 'You think you could tell me about my mother? The woman you married?'

'Of course. With the greatest of pleasure, Big Feller.' And then he promptly vanished. *Bastard!*

*

I had another trouble-free night, devoid of sounds and disturbances. If this carried on, I really would have no more need for Michael. We came back from Mandy's Caff the next day to find a note under the door. 'Call me. I have news,' it read.

I instantly knew what it was. Myrna had cancelled. She wouldn't be able to travel after all. I was back in, the Pink Palace beckoned with flashing Christmas lights. Without waiting to phone, I ran up the High Street to Richard Woking Estates. Janine looked up in surprise.

'She's not coming, is she?'

'Oh Sanjay, get off me! People will see.'

'Never bothered you before, did it?'

'This is broad daylight.'

'So, tell me.'

'What? Myrna? Of course she's coming. Tomorrow.'

'Then? What did you want me for?'

'You didn't have to come all this way. You could have called me. I have an offer on the ground floor flat.'

There we were again. I had the same sensation as before, when the money had first come through. As if the blood in my body had stopped pumping for a moment. Like sitting in the back of a long black car the split second before it goes *whoosh!* with a quantum leap that blasts you into the next dimension.

'Don't get too excited. The offer is only at 13,500. Way below asking. I'm working on them. It's a difficult sale as you know. Your workmanship . . .' She looked at me covertly to see how I was taking the criticism. I registered the foxy look on her face, but my mind was a million miles away, in Ilminster Gardens.

'Janine,' I said, struggling to find the words, as if I were talking to a stranger. 'Are we still good?'

'Good? What do you mean good?'

'I mean . . . what we had. Is it still there?'

'Why wouldn't it be? Don't be a child, Sanjay. The future is a blank page. You can't start writing on it till you get there. So keep turning the pages.' She began to laugh, a little patronizingly. For once, I wasn't laughing along.

'Keep tomorrow night free. Myrna's taking us all out to dinner. I've booked a table at the Golden Curry for eight. And you better behave yourself. She'll be watching us like the alcohol police on Poya day.'

18

The manholes are built, the peaks and troughs of the channels inside flawlessly rendered in cement by Sean, with the practised hand of a pastry cook.

'You missed your vocation, mate,' I say. 'You have a great future in some bakery, icing cakes all day.'

'Fuck off, you bastard,' he replies good-naturedly.

We fill up the system with water and watch with consternation as the water levels fall yet again. There is still a leak, a minute one, but enough to fail the test. The thought of having to dig it all up fills me with a terror too nightmarish to contemplate.

And happy, happy Mr Malachy is coming tomorrow. What are we going to tell him?

I hear steps overhead. Two pairs of feet. 'Sanjay? Big Feller?'

I run up the ladder-like steps of the cellar and hurl myself into her arms. She steps back to take a look at me. 'My goodness, how you have changed! Where did all this hair come from?'

I flush with pride. The way a son must, the day his mother finally acknowledges his manhood. I look at her as she stands there with Janak. She too has changed—though I don't remark on it. She has aged; this funeral has been the death of all of us. All except the dead man himself who is looking younger than ever; in his preternatural prime, in fact.

I take Myrna on a tour of my little empire, and I have to admit it is looking quite good: the not-so-crooked-now wallpaper, the midnight-blue bath, the MFI kitchen—a far cry from Clifford Road. *Please God, let these flats find buyers before Mr Jurisevicz flattens me with his iron fist.* The first and last Asian builder of the Western world expired under tragic Polish circumstances. RIP. Xkrrh.

'Will you come to Mandy's Caff for a workman's breakfast? A proper no-holds-barred fry-up?'

She shakes her head. 'I'll join you tomorrow. Janak is cooking up a curry for me today.'

'Goat?'

'How did you know?'

'I'll see you all at the restaurant tonight,' I tell her. 'Can't wait!'

'Neither can I,' she says, looking at me with tender suspicion, the way an excise inspector might look at a lovable old neighbourhood bootlegger.

After she goes, I return to the horror awaiting me in the cellar. 'The new pipes, the terracotta, must be absorbing the water,' Sean says.

'But so much?'

He shakes his head, stroking the few blond wisps of incipient beard on his chin. Finally he says, 'Let's cheat.'

'Cheat? You? A good Catholic boy?'

'Oh, we're the worst,' he says grinning in delight.

'How will you do it?'

'Here, let me show you.'

He empties the system, reaches inside the drainpipe as far as his hand will go and blocks it, with one of the black and white Frisbees. When he refills the manhole, it appears that the whole system is still under test, though in fact only the manhole is now full. Mr Malachy will never know. He does not look like the sort of man to put his lily-white hands into someone else's sewer. Or so we pray. We leave the manhole full for the rest of the day. The water levels don't drop even a hundredth of an inch.

Sean opens the front door. He cups his hands around his mouth and shouts down the empty echoing street, 'You can swim in it if you like, Mr Malachy!'

*

I watch Janine stride across Clapham High Street—her glorious hair loose like a black river in flood, her black boots riding thigh-high. I know her usual office attire, and the change is startling. I know, too, that this is not for the benefit of us men—certainly not for me—but for the other woman in the party, her ex-sister-in-law.

'You look smashing,' I manage to whisper before we enter the restaurant.

So here we are, gathered at the Golden Curry, Myrna's extended family (even though she may not be fully aware of this fact): her son, Janak, with his partner, George, her prospective son-in-law; me, her adoptive son; and Janine, her ex-sister-in-law, who is in great danger of becoming her adoptive *daughter-in-law* if I have anything to do with it. A typical Sri Lankan family in other words, of the don't-ask-don't-tell variety; where everything is understood yet nothing is understood.

'Here, Big Feller, come sit next to my sister-in-law,' Myrna says, the opening gambit in her starring role as agent provocateur. 'Have you two met before?'

'Janine is handling the sale of my flats.'

'A purely professional relationship,' Janine adds.

'My, Janine, what a complete *pro* you have become.'

Janak pats the seat next to him. 'I think Sanjay should come to this side and sit next to George, his *special* friend.' This is news to me, the specialness of George, but I am willing to go along with it for the sake of World Peace. I can see Myrna's antennae quivering.

'*Special*? Really? How did the two of you meet?'

'Ask him,' George says. 'The *naughty* boy.'

Myrna looks sharply at the pair of us. *Has she been missing something here?*

The moon-faced maître d' is beaming at us like, well, a full moon on Poya day. I notice that the pictures of the Taj Mahal are encircled by Santas—flashing purple, red, green—and I wonder idly which cash-and-carry they both shop at, the owner of this restaurant and Bilquis. And there, underneath the Taj Mahal, I can see my father, the flashing Santas forming a pretty halo around the hologram of his head. The party is complete.

'Myrna, how long are you here for?' Janine asks.

'That's what Janak asked me just now. What's wrong with you people? Trying to get rid of me already?'

No one laughs. It is too close to the truth.

'Stay as long as you like. The flat is entirely at your disposal.' Without asking anyone's permission, Janine lights a cigarette. This is 1980. No permission needed to light up in a crowded restaurant, but I have never seen her smoke before. The strain is already beginning to tell.

'You can move in with me the day she gets tired of you,' I joke gamely, lamely.

At this point my father leans over. 'Ask her, Sanjay. Ask her why the food was so horrible at my funeral.'

'Shh!' I hiss. Everyone looks at me. 'Sorry, something in my nose,' I explain. George hands me a tissue. Helpful, special George. Ever-ready with a tissue.

The maître d' brings in the food, mountains of it.

'Myrna, you're spoiling us,' I say.

'Anything is better than your cooking, Myrna,' my father adds, whispering in her ear. 'You know I had to die to get away from it?'

At the end of the evening we're all gathered on the pavement outside—in the freezing cold—for the next half hour, without which no Sri Lankan goodbye is ever complete.

'And where do you live?' Myrna asks George innocently.

George thinks quickly. 'North of the river,' he says.

'Perhaps you'd like to walk him to the tube station, Big Feller?'

'George is old enough to go on his own!' I snap.

Myrna is like a dog with a new bone in her mouth, shaking her head experimentally from side to side, running all over the house wagging her tail. She has cleared Janine of all suspicion, but now she has a fresh obsession. I could kill Janak.

'I will walk him home,' Janak offers nobly. 'You never know, he might get mugged on his own, poor boy.'

The women head off up to the bus stop on Clapham Common, the three men downhill in the opposite direction, my father a silent fourth at my elbow.

'Lovely woman,' says George. 'So refined. Such good breeding, such *perfect* manners.'

My father makes retching noises. 'Behave!' I growl.

Janak and George look at me, puzzled and hurt.

I would love to tell them that my idiot father has risen from the dead to plague me. I could do with a bit of moral support here, some reassurance that I am not cracking up, that it is perfectly normal to have a Sri Lankan psychical sidekick following you around. (Never leave home without one.) I fear it would be the end of my friendship with them. It would be like telling them I had Ebola or something. Though frankly I would have preferred the Ebola any day.

'You were not very nice to Myrna, were you?' I tell my father when we get back home. I recognize his killer instincts, which sadly do not seem to have died with his death. Always go after the one who is your biggest threat: demolish them first and the rest will be easy. Since his death Myrna seems to have taken charge, directing the other Satellites, doggedly pursuing me to save me from myself. My father sees this clearly; he has trained his guns on her accordingly.

'You ought to be ashamed of yourself. She fed us for most of our lives. Now she's come all this way to check up on me, purely out of respect for you. All you can do is criticize her cooking.'

'Pah!'

He does not feel guilty. It seems ghosts don't do guilt, particularly not this one.

'You know, your girl isn't bad?' he says after a while. 'I could go for her myself.'

'Who, Janine? Apparently you did. Apparently you didn't come up to the mark.'

'Hah! Is that what she's telling everyone now?'

This conversation has gone on long enough, and like all conversations with my father, it is going nowhere.

'I'm off to bed,' I say. 'Try not to haunt Michael on your way out.'

*

'I have not seen such a water-tight system in a long time,' remarked Mr Malachy with great remorse. 'You must be commended on a job well done.'

We were standing with our mugs of tea in the cellar, watching the water levels. Sadly, Douglas was not on site today to lift us out of ourselves.

'I have failed so many drains around here,' Mr Malachy said wistfully. 'This one I might have to pass.' He gave me his mug. 'Can you hold this for me please?'

Then he took a pristine white handkerchief from his pocket and spread it carefully on the floor by the manhole, lowering himself on to it with difficulty. (Sean and I were wetting ourselves by now.) He ran his fingers around the brickwork. 'Tasty,' he said, with almost a sob. 'Tasty piece of work.' He stayed there in that kneeling position, contemplating; without doubt the worst ten seconds of my life.

Then he got up and our troubles were over.

'I will issue the certificate on Monday morning. Goodbye,' he added tearfully. 'And good luck.'

Sean and I laughed and laughed, hugging each other in relief.

*

There is a thin watery sun today, coating the grey streets with a pale lemony, detergent-like wash of colour. The radios are on, the ladders out on every site in the neighbourhood. On the streets the inhabitants are dressed in bright primary colours. With a little wilful myopia and a whole lot of imagination you can even convince yourself that you are in some resort of the northern tropics. I am glad that Brixton and Clapham North are putting their best foot forward for Myrna. We are in the smoky confines of Mandy's Caff.

'Phyllis, Rani, Kamala, all send their love. They miss you and want you back.' She pauses. Then she says innocently, as if this fresh thought has only just struck her: 'Actually, when *are* you coming back?'

'Depends on how this business goes, Myrna. Janine may have found me a buyer. We'll know better in the next day or two.'

'Janine?' I see her go rigid on the other side of the table. 'Have you tried putting the flats on with other agents? I'm sure there are plenty around here.'

At this point I could so easily lie, but I don't. 'I've decided to give her sole agency.'

She begins to shake her head, her old fears returning. 'Be very careful, Big Feller.'

'What? You think she's going to seduce me, ruin me in some way?' I laugh, a booming stage laugh.

'Don't joke, Big Feller. You're young and inexperienced. You don't know how these things work.' Then she scents the fresh bone she dug up last night. 'Tell me *all* about George,' she says roguishly.

At this point Mandy comes up to us, a signal honour because she normally never leaves her place behind the counter. In fact, I have often wondered whether she has legs.

'Would your mother like a piece of my cherry pie? On the house?'

Myrna flushes with pride and all talk of George is temporarily forgotten. After a bite or two of the pie—deliciously gooey and drowning in lashings of vanilla ice cream—she returns to the subject.

'I know how you boys like to have . . . to have an innocent bit of fun now and then. But think of the family name. What would your father say?'

'Faggot! Poofter!' says my father quite loudly. 'That's what your father would say!' I am amazed no one can hear him.

'I'm okay, Myrna,' I say gently, putting my hand over hers on the table. 'I can look after myself. And I'll come back when I'm good and ready.'

She looks troubled but doesn't say anything more as I walk her back through those dishwasher-bright streets. I don't tell her that I have decided to stay in England till I am thirty. She would die of distress.

PART III

19

A full fortnight after the funeral, I managed to evict the last of the hangers-on, a very distant and elderly cousin of my father's called Mark Anthony. I took him down to Fort Railway Station to catch the intercity back to Kandy. When we got to the station he found, unaccountably, that he had no change for the taxi, so I paid. I bought a platform ticket and saw him to his seat on the train, a first-class air-conditioned observation car seat. Unfortunately, the seat assigned to him was right next to the lavatory compartment, the odour issuing from which was somewhat robust.

Mark Anthony gave me a baleful look.

'I'm sorry,' I said. I wasn't quite sure why I was apologizing on behalf of the Ceylon Government Railways, but it was apparently my fault.

He pressed a note on me. 'Take this. No, please, I insist. Louis would have wanted you to have it.'

I looked at the filthy, much-handled note. It was twenty rupees, the equivalent of thirty pence those days. 'Thank you. But really, this is way too much.'

When I got back home they were waiting for me, the Satellites of Love, assembled around the table. The transistor which had been cleared away these past few weeks to make room for the funeral festivities had been brought back, a silent tabernacle in the centre, exuding a strong sacramental vibe.

'Big Feller, we have come to a decision. We think you need to get away. Go abroad.'

'So you're trying to get rid of me now, are you?'

'A change of skies will do you good.'

'What makes you think I wasn't planning to go anyway?'

'If you stay here—the way your father had it planned—you'll get stale. After a while you won't want to go anywhere. You'll be trapped within your unhappiness.'

'What if I never come back?'

I could see the look of pain on their faces. *Was this what they had feared, each one of them, with my father? That he would go away and leave them?* It melted my heart to see that they were able to rise above these fears and advise me to go all the same, because it might be the best thing for me.

After I had shooed them out of the house with the greatest difficulty, I opened the door to my father's room. Mark Anthony had commandeered it till now, in his position as the eldest male relative. The paraphernalia of death—the cannulas and catheters, the bedpans and enema tubes, the iron hook on which the saline bottle had hung and the air mattress for prevention of bedsores—all had been cleared away, donated to the cancer hospital. The room was almost as it had been when he was well.

I opened his pedimented jackwood almirah, something I would never have dreamt of doing while he was alive because he guarded his privacy so fiercely. I saw neatly hanging the made-in-Bristol suits, and the row of leather shoes accordioned after a lifetime of use, and I was hit by a blast of his very existence: as in those brief seconds when an express train speeds past, in the opposite direction, sucking the air out of your compartment. And the grief in my body was expelled by that blast, leaving me breathless, faint, weak in the legs. I held on to the wine-dark wood to stay upright.

In the middle section of the almirah were two drawers. I opened the upper one and there, on top, as if he had wanted me to see it, was a brown envelope. Inside was a black-and-white snapshot. Two children against the front door of a house, a girl and a boy. Even though the photo was black-and-white you could tell it was high summer: there was something about their features—open to the sky like flowers to the sun—that spoke of the air around them, heavy with the scent of honeysuckle and rose. I ran my finger around the crinkled white edge and turned it over.

'Philip and Domenica Gaisford, Alleyn Court,' it said on the back. 'Zeal Monachorum, 1931.'

He had never shown me this snap before, never for a moment imagined I might want to see it. To see where my mother had come from, to see where her story had begun, all those years ago. My hands were shaking and I found my grief replaced by rage, instant and blind, red-hot and murderous. I slammed the drawer shut and left the room.

*

'Don't get too excited,' Janine said. 'I think I've talked the buyers into coming up to the asking price.'

'What? 15,000?'

'They need a few little things done. Could you repaint the back room?'

'With pleasure.'

'And please don't get angry. You think someone might be able to re-tile the bathroom?' She laughed so loud that it didn't leave me any room for self-pity.

'Their valuer will come along next week. I've told them a fib—that someone else is after it too, so they have to move pretty sharpish.'

Another week, another surveyor.

I asked Sean, 'Have you ever tiled before?'

'Only the wife's kitchen.'

'Fancy having a go? Since you're so brilliant at icing cakes?'

'Fuck off.'

'I'll take that as a yes, then?'

*

That evening I invited Myrna home to Tintern Street with Janak.

'Your friend not here?' she asked innocently.

I got annoyed. 'You know, Myrna, he's not a close friend. He lives miles away!' (He was, in fact, just around the corner, secreted in the attic at Bedford Road.)

'What a shame,' she said. 'I mean for you.' She looked round. 'Marvellous job you've done here, Big Feller. Who would have thought you had it in you?'

'Who indeed?' said my father loudly. 'Certainly not me.'

'Oh, shut your gob!'

'Sanjay don't speak to me like that. London's made you lose your manners.'

'Gosh, Myrna, sorry. I didn't mean it like that! It just sort of slipped out.' I leant over and kissed her powdered, rose-watered cheek, and she was somewhat mollified.

I set out the mismatched plates and assorted cutlery on the kitchen table, and unpacked the takeaway from the Golden Curry for my first-ever dinner party. It was fitting that my first guest be Myrna. I had taken care to get her her favourite drink, sweet martini and lemonade.

At ten sharp, Michael rolled in. He stood at the doorway swaying wildly, looking at the three of us.

'Oh God, they're multiplying!' he said despairingly.

I was the only one familiar with Michael's very decided views on immigrants and immigration. 'You can talk,' I said annoyed. 'Weren't you married to one of us?'

He looked at me cunningly. 'Big mistake, weren't it? Only good for one thing she was—'

'Too much information,' I said getting to my feet. 'I think we'd better call it a day.'

Michael followed us out into the corridor. 'Rivers of blood,' he said wagging his finger at Myrna's departing rear, generously upholstered in crimplene. '*There will be rivers of blood!*'

'I wouldn't worry about him,' my father said later in the bedroom. 'It's quite usual. The most recent wave of immigrants is always the most racist. Lock the door behind you once you've got in yourself so no one else can follow. Keep all the pleasures of martyrdom to yourself.'

'Since when did you become such an expert on racism?' I snapped.

'Isn't it time you got rid of him?'

'Why? Because you're my minder now?'

'Sanjay, Sanjay. I don't think you have any idea what danger you're in. Michael too.'

'Oh really? Then fuck off downstairs and do a bit of minding while I try to get some sleep.'

As if my father had taken him aside and cautioned him that night itself, Michael came upstairs next morning. 'Can I have the week off?'

'Why? You have something better to do?'

'Who knows?' he said with ponderous good humour.

Myrna was around for quite a bit longer. It wasn't likely that I would be spending any nights away from the site till she left, so I could afford to spare Michael. 'Go ahead,' I said. 'Only a week, though, okay?'

That morning I ran up the High Street to get two more cans of Disco. For Sean I chose some four-inch square tiles in plain white. When in doubt stick to white, I said to myself, sounding a little like Michael himself. Back home I began painting. I could see what the problem was. The room was freshly plastered, and in my enthusiasm and ignorance I had painted the top coat without first using an oil-based primer. It was too late to do anything about it now except slap on more emulsion, hoping the walls would turn a perfect white with no discolouration showing through.

Painting away, I thought of my father's words. *Was I in such great danger? Surely the unearthly events of the past month had perfectly rational explanations to them? He's just jealous of Michael.* With my father, it had always had to be about him. In death now, as in life.

It was almost unbelievable how this creature—there was no better word I could think of—had become so much a part of my new life. I was no longer freaking out at every appearance of this unholy hallucination, this metaphysical monstrosity.

'I am here only because you want me here.' Had I conjured him up? If so, why at this particular moment in England? Why not back then in Sri Lanka?

'To ward off the others,' he had said. *So who were these others?* I went back to my painting. And the sheer slip-slop of the brush, the hypnotic effect of repetition, was enough to calm my troubled mind.

The buyers, a young couple, came that afternoon. Nobody told me they were the buyers, but from the proprietorial looks they were already giving the bricks and mortar I could tell.

'Unusual design,' the man said. 'A weird sort of geometry I can't quite get my head around. Odd volumes. As if some mad mathematician had designed it.'

'It's quirky,' she agreed. 'I like it.'

'Shame about the decor!' they said in unison. They looked at me guiltily and giggled.

Janine brought around a succession of people, taking them to look at the upstairs without even a glance at me. After tea, I could wait no longer and went around to my office. I told Bilquis about the ground floor offer. 'Yay!' she said punching the air with a clenched fist, her glass bangles click-clacking down to her elbow. I had lived all my 'professional' life at the coin box telephone in this shop and she had lived it vicariously through me: my victories were hers; my defeats too.

'Any news?' I asked Janine when she answered.

'I have not one but two offers on the upstairs. I am playing one off against the other.'

This tactic—which seemed so offensive to us at the time, strait-laced and conventional as we were—was to become standard practice in the property boom of the '80s, introducing the word 'gazumping' into our vocabulary.

My troubles, it seemed, were about to end. Overcome with emotion, I said into the phone without thinking, 'I love you.'

'Love?' she said scornfully. 'Don't be absurd. What would *you* know! You're just a child.'

Instinctively I looked to see if Bilquis was listening. She must have seen the marks of pain across my face, striated and flickering like a campfire in the dark. She looked away. When I left, she gave me a tin of jackfruit pieces as a sort of consolation prize.

*

'Come back soon,' Myrna said, stroking my hair.

Her time in England was up. She did not really have anything particular to return to, but I could see how she had come to realize that this was not the life for her. Janak and I had seen as much of her as we were able to: no one here in the Western world had time to spare, to sit and just *be* with anyone else, drinking endless cups of tea. We were all victims of some invisible timetable ordering our every movement, governing our every step. It was a timetable that Myrna would never comprehend or be willing to be governed by, unless she got a job of her own and settled into the system herself. I could see the puzzlement on her face; why anyone in their right mind might consider it necessary to submit to such an order.

She was in that position that so many Sri Lankans found themselves, of not having enough to live lavishly or extravagantly, yet having more than enough to survive. I too had been in that state till I came here. I realized that that sort of middle path was better practised in a country which was more open to it: a country like ours, where the fine art of merely surviving has been raised to such a pitch of perfection, by people like my father and the Satellites. Myrna might see how a life lived more comprehensively than hers might lead to more fulfilment. She did not see the necessity of living such a life; even if she did not resent the likes of Janak and me who did.

'I might be back sooner than you think,' I said jovially, 'if the flats don't sell and they throw me out as a failure.' I knew though that I was being disingenuous. The race had long begun; I could already feel myself pulling ahead.

I embraced her, subsumed momentarily in the rosewater-infused aura of a world I was fast forgetting—like the sleeper who throws the duvet over his head one last time to keep in the warmth, knowing the alarm will sound its final call any minute, and he will have to get up to face the realities of his working day.

The last thing she said to me was: 'Look after my son. I think he needs more looking after than you.'

What did she mean by that? I have often wondered. *Did she have any inkling of the exotic and recondite tropical jungle in which prowled his private life?* I longed to tell her about George, but those were not my secrets to give away. So I hugged her in wordless thanks for the nonpareil job she had always performed—unquestioning and silent—the job of being my mother.

*

'Thank God she's gone,' my father said. 'She was beginning to get on my nerves.'

'You know, you're the most homophobic, woman-hating bastard it has ever been my pleasure to meet?'

'Thank you, Sanjay. The praise is entirely undeserved. Though I can tell you it's not easy—swimming against this, this *tsunami* of political correctness.' He was positively preening himself like a cat in the sun. 'Now can we get on with the business of getting you out of this house and into the next?'

'The next?'

'You're not stopping here, are you? You'd better start house-hunting immediately so you're ready when the money comes through.'

This was a side of my father I had never encountered before: the property tycoon ghost; a welcome change from the class-one bitch ghost. There wasn't much work left on site—a little bit of decoration to complete while I waited for the valuer of the lower flat—so I spent the morning on a blitz of local agents, as I had done three months ago (though that seemed like a lifetime ago now!). If the two sales came through, I would have a sizeable chunk of cash—over 15,000 pounds—to play around with.

I went back to Mr Nikolaos of NatWest; in my workman's overalls this time, not bothering to change, with paint in my nails, plaster dust in my hair. The colourful paisley tie that flourished on Mr Nikolaos's chest was like a loud voice in an empty room now, speaking to no one. Certainly not to me. But he must have smelt the odour of money I was unconsciously giving off because he received me like a long-lost brother. I now had a golden track record. No one loves you like a banker who no longer has to take a risk on you.

Mr Nikolaos explained that he would be delighted to finance me, that he could offer me a loan to the limit of thirty thousand pounds, an awful lot of money those days. Not only that, but he would arrange a bridging loan so that Charterfield Investments could be paid off as soon as the ground-floor flat had exchanged contracts. I could then go ahead and buy pretty much whatever I wanted.

Behind Mr Nikolaos I could see my father putting his thumbs up in jubilation. He bent down, putting his ghostly face right up against Mr Nikolaos's rather florid one. 'You know, Mr Nikolaos,' he said sweetly. 'You are such a fucking hypocrite?'

20

'Well, this is certainly an interesting flat, Mr . . . Mr?'

'de Silva,' I said. 'Would you like a cup of tea?'

'If there's one going.'

I made him a mug of PG Tips and sat with him at the kitchen table. 'I'm sorry it's not Ceylon tea,' I said apologetically. 'Though I suppose that might be construed as a bribe.'

He wasn't going to do much surveying as far as I could see, this surveyor. It was only later that I learnt that banks and building societies lending money to young buyers were only interested in the value of the property, not its structural condition. They knew something of which we were only dimly aware back then: that the price of these flats was actually going up by the minute. In the eight weeks it would take for the sale to complete, the value of the flat would already have shot up by a few thousand pounds. The market was at the start of a bull run that would take it almost to the end of the eighties. It was impossible to lose.

When the valuer had left, apparently quite satisfied with the set-up, I phoned Janine to give her the low-down.

'The buyers want to exchange before Christmas and complete early in the new year,' she told me.

'I have an idea,' I said. 'Hear me out. Shall we go somewhere for Christmas? Let me take you away on holiday.'

'I can't talk now. I have clients in the office. Later.'

With Myrna's departure, I had moved back in. I never again mentioned those fateful three words—*I love you*—that had so inopportunely slipped out, like baby food from a toddler's mouth. I had been too busy banging the spoon to realize their gravity then. I was embarrassed even to think about it now.

'Let's go somewhere warm,' I said that night. 'Let's go to Sri Lanka.'

'Are you mad? We've only just got over Myrna's suspicions.'

'We don't have to see her, do we?'

'What exactly are you suggesting?'

'Let's stay in a hotel. Let's go incognito, as tourists; not bother with family.'

'Incognito? You must be crazier than you look. Remember this is Sri Lanka we're talking about? They don't do incognito over there, in case you've forgotten. It's an alien concept.'

Well, I had at least put the idea into her head. It was a start.

*

The house I finally settled on was 86, Strathleven Road, on the other side of Acre Lane, more towards the heartlands of Brixton. It was small and would produce, if I played my cards right, two modest one-bed flats. The asking price was low and I could comfortably finish the work within my budget. More importantly—and I never thought I would hear myself saying this—it got my father's seal of approval. He stood in the corridor and sucked in the air, swilling it around appreciatively like a wine taster. I almost expected him to say 'strong notes of black currant and violets with a cheeky soupçon of ghost'.

Instead he said, 'Not bad. I sense less here.'

'Less what?'

'Less of the others.'

If all went well, I could start sometime in the new year.

'I'm sorry it isn't one of yours,' I told Janine. She made a little noise in her throat signifying that it didn't matter, but I could tell she was upset. 'I'll give you sole agency when they're ready, okay?'

I took Sean, Jo, Douglas and the Mulrooneys around to give estimates. 'Would you like a day job?' I asked Michael that evening. 'A bit of labouring work, if there's any going?' I still intended to do much of it myself, but an extra pair of hands would help. And I now had the money.

'Don't mind if I do,' he replied.

We had had time to get used to each other's odd behaviour: I his drunken racist views, pig-ignorant for the most part but ultimately well-meant I am sure; he the shouting he must have heard from my bedroom every night as I cursed and swore at my in-house ghost. He always made sure to leave by seven in the morning, well before the workers arrived. Was he ashamed of this job? Was he ashamed to be seen working for an Asian? Then I remembered that he had once been married to an Asian woman, so it couldn't have been that.

'What do you really want out of life, Michael?' I once asked, when we were down to the last quarter of our nightly bottle.

He shrugged. Perhaps what he really wanted was acceptance by the rest of the Mulrooneys. They had turned up in the new country and become 'civilized'. Being the eldest, he had never seen the need for this, having to give up the old ways as an essential prerequisite to being absorbed into the new. Seeing him I understood how each and every immigrant must make the choice for himself. There were no clear answers. All you knew was that you could not keep two clashing identities hanging like suits in a cupboard, changing them at will. At one point you had to make your choice; one that stuck with you for the rest of your life. Even if you made no conscious move in either direction, the choice was frequently made for you—in the food you ate, the company you kept, your clothes, even the way your accent veered despite your best efforts at keeping it constant.

*

That evening, I met up with Janak and George at the pub for a post-mortem—post-Myrna—drink. My father disapproved of their relationship, the great liberal he had professed to be in life having become, unaccountably, this die-hard, reactionary, Trump-voting sort of ghost.

'Move with the times,' I told him. 'Learn to accept people for who they are.'

'Hah! Over my dead body. Get it? Dead body?' He hung around the pub for a while, making homophobic comments, trying to get a rise out of me, but I had learnt to control my tongue in company. After a while he vanished.

'Here's to us,' Janak said raising his mug. 'For a successful and convincing performance.'

The beer must have given me some sort of spurious courage because I said, 'Isn't it time you told her? You're over thirty now.'

'Look, I'm never going to go back, right? She's never here for any great length of time when she comes. I reckon I have at least a couple of years before she decides to visit again. Why give her unnecessary grief?' He looked at me shrewdly through half-closed eyes. 'And you're a right one to talk, aren't you?'

I made no comment. Being in a relationship with a married woman almost old enough to be my mother was just as great a sin in Sri Lankan eyes. I could imagine the unhappiness I would cause by taking Janine to meet the Satellites. Far easier to keep her under wraps; the coward's way out, the Sri Lankan way.

The real puzzle here was my father. He seemed to have come to terms with my seeing Janine. In fact he was rather proud of it, truth be told; the way one man might envy another his sexual exploits. Marriage, I was sure, would be a different matter entirely. But hang on a minute. *Who said anything about marriage?* That night I stayed at Tintern, being too drunk to make my way to Janine's. My father was nowhere to be seen. I am sure the house smelt like a winery with Michael downstairs and me upstairs.

I woke up in the morning to the sound of running water. Michael had gone home. In the bathroom upstairs, the bath was filled to the level of the overflow. *And the taps were still on.* Michael never came up, so it could not have been him. I had been way too drunk last night to go anywhere near the bath. Had the pressure in the taps been greater, the water would have spilled over the rim and through the floorboards, destroying the plaster ceiling below. I had been extremely lucky.

The worst thing was that there was nobody I could tell all this to. In Sri Lanka, these happenings would have been treated with the greatest gravity, welcomed even: everyone had their transcendental tale, their tame-ghost story, forming part of the private family archive. Here in the cold world of reason, there seemed to be no room for the eccentricities of the occult.

That afternoon a man came and nailed an 'Under Offer' sign across the 'For Sale' board. Bilquis was standing outside the house surveying the goings-on. 'You done well then, love?' She looked surprised and gratified. The lab rat had outperformed his scientist's wildest expectations. (Breaking news: the parameters of subcontinental entrepreneurism might have to be rewritten.)

'Come in, I'll give you a little tour.'

'Oh no, I don't think so!' She shivered.

I was disappointed at not being able to show off my brilliant handiwork to a fellow Asian.

'Bilquis,' I said. 'How well did you know Mr Brown?'

'Well enough, love. Well enough to know not to mess with him.'

'You know there's something odd—'

'Don't want to know, love.' She held up her hand in warning. 'Not my business.'

It was curious how we immigrants seemed to have imported this other preternatural world of shadows with us, planting it in the stony ground of rationality, where against all odds it had taken root and flourished. Perhaps there were sympathetic ears to be had after all. I had just not found them yet.

I walked back with Bilquis to the telephone.

'The top flat is under offer,' Janine said. 'Asking price.'

Again, I felt the seismic shift under my feet, heard the rumble of the earth, as if a great transporter were changing gears.

'Is the work complete?'

'Almost. The flats are ready for occupation. I only have to move Michael out.'

'Michael?'

'The watcher.'

That evening my father travelled with me on the No. 37 bus to Clapham Junction. I told him about the open bath tap, and the water almost overflowing.

'We aren't out of the woods yet,' he said grimly. 'When do you move into the new place?'

'Some time in the new year.'

I got off at Arding and Hobbs. He followed me all the way up Ilminster Gardens, hovering behind me as I rang the buzzer. I turned around. 'Good night,' I said firmly. After a few lingering seconds he took the hint. The psychic sicko.

*

Janine had spread herself out on the bed, a glossy magazine open in front of her.

'Oh, goody,' I said. 'Another manual. What are we trying out tonight? Is it your turn with the paddle or mine?'

'Stop it, you filthy, disgusting boy. I'm trying to choose a holiday for us. How does seven nights at the InterContinental sound, flights and half board for 645 pounds?'

'Done. I'm an easy guy to please. Now put that away.'

'I'm still worried though. What if your old women see us?'

'You're selling my flats, aren't you? You're my business partner.'

'You know, for a Sri Lankan born and bred, you're a little simple-minded? You think people will believe that story?'

'Rich old men travel with their "nieces" all the time. Why can't a young man travel with his "auntie"?'

'Doesn't work like that, does it?' she said sadly.

'Anyway I don't want people thinking of you as some sort of sugar mummy. You're my partner. If they don't like it, they can fuck off.'

She remained silent.

'Look,' I said, cupping her face in my hands. 'Let's go and enjoy ourselves, right? Don't overthink it.'

21

'It hasn't happened yet,' the solicitor explains patiently. 'I told you, exchange of contracts is set for Tuesday morning, 20 December. Completion twenty-eight days later, on 17 January.'

'Thank you, Mr Cooper. I'll call you on Tuesday.'

Bilquis lets out a sigh of disappointment. 'Lawyers,' she says.

Refusing her kind offer of a tin of rambutan to calm the nerves, I make my way out into the streets. I realize much later that this strange limbo I am in is a regular part of the builder's life. Periods of total inaction—waiting till the flats are sold—followed by an eight-week sprint as soon as the next house becomes available. It suits the dual nature of my personality: the frenzied Asian labourer buzzing like an energetic fly, hacking mindlessly at concrete with his club hammer to the amusement of his fellow workers; alternating every few months with the degenerate islander surrendering silently to his sybaritic pink pleasures, entire weekends spent in bed, eating baked beans off a tray when the occasional need arises.

I walk up the High Street avoiding Janine's side of the road altogether. She would not thank me for occupying space in her small office, wasting her time on a working day. I cross over to the Common at the top of the road. I am a shapeless mass in an Oxfam overcoat joining other shapeless masses—almost all of them elderly—buffeted along by the hostile winds that rage across those bleak spaces, below the dishonest glimmer of a fish-scale sky.

I anchor my weight to a bench, asking myself: *How has it been so far? How is life treating you now?*

I am so far removed, both physically and emotionally, from what I left behind in Sri Lanka. A life that was stuck in a swamp of self-doubt and apathy, controlled by the whims and fancies of a capricious old man, to whom it gave endless pleasure to order us all about—me and the Satellites—dressing us in the shabby clothes of that second-hand life he had ordained for us. Is this unfair? Maybe. I am still too close to those events to take a rational call. I am a prisoner of the recent past awaiting fair trial, one who will have spent so long in jail before his case comes up that perhaps, just perhaps, he will be let off unscarred and scot-free when the day finally arrives.

As if I have willed it, my father appears on the bench next to me. I look at him in amusement. 'Speak of the devil!'

'Don't insult me,' he says giving me that sly sideways look of his. 'Cold enough for you then?'

I burrow further into my coat.

'I hear you're off to warm Sri Lanka? Give them my love, won't you?'

'You're not coming then?'

'First rule of modern metaphysics. We others cannot cross water.'

'So how did you get here in the first place?'

'That's the whole point, see. We're only allowed one port of call.'

'You mean the day I go home I'm free of you forever?'

'Sanjay,' he says, '*Sanjay*. At least have the decency to fake a little sadness. Why do you think I'm moving heaven and earth to make your building projects here a success?'

'Guilt. You're feeling guilty at having stifled me all these years.'

'I think this Janine woman seems to be quite good for you.'

'Really? That's a change. I thought you'd be the first to say how unsuitable she was.'

'She's made a man of you. We must be grateful to her.' He looks at me, his lip curling involuntarily. I wait with bitter years of experience for the punchline. 'With a face like yours there aren't a whole lot of options, are there?'

Then, because I am curious, I ask: 'What about children? Kids' birthday parties, musical chairs, patties, cutlets? Some rich young girl? Isn't that the future you had planned for me?'

There is a woman not far from us, rooting about in a trash bin, hurling out empty crisp packets and beer cans in a frenzy, searching for hidden treasure. We watch this for a while. My father's saying nothing. I'm playing the picador now, sticking the lance into the bull's neck, drawing a thin trail of blood, attempting to goad him into rage. 'If I stay with Janine, you'll have no grandchildren, will you? End of the line.' I draw a finger across my throat.

He shrugs. 'Do I care?'

Who is this man? Will someone please tell me what they have done with the man formerly known as My Father? All these things—the unbroken line of descent, the successor to carry on the family name—have always meant a lot to any Sri Lankan male.

'You're not the man you used to be,' I say pityingly. I want to provoke him so he will rant and roar, fight back ferociously, but he doesn't. I should be happy with this apathy. Instead, I am inexplicably sorry. 'That whole Sri Lankan thing would have mattered a lot to you in the old days, wouldn't it?'

'For sure. But I'm dead now, aren't I? I think you'll find, Sanjay, that death has made me *quite* broad-minded. Philosophical too.'

Later, after he has vanished, I think to myself: Perhaps it is true. Perhaps death has mellowed him. Perhaps he really is prepared to sacrifice his principles to pay this ransom price, the one that will buy me my happiness. I am possessed with a sudden, unbearable joy.

My father accepts me! But don't get ahead of yourself, mate. It's only a goddam ghost, isn't it?

Yet I leave the park bench with a lightness to my step, and in my heart an unreasonable, unexpected happiness—like the uninvited guest that just slipped into your house while you were away for a moment, whom you find in the kitchen upon your return, cozily drinking your tea and eating your biscuits.

*

The exchange of contracts took place as planned on the morning of the twentieth. By afternoon the bridging loan had come into play, settling Charterfield Investments with Mr Nikolaos's NatWest money. I was free of Mr Jurisevicz forever.

'Yay!' said Bilquis. 'Yay!'

With great difficulty I dissuaded her from calling Mr Jurisevicz anonymously to say 'Xkrrh!' loudly down the phone. We compromised by opening a can of jackfruit pieces, sharing it with a common plastic fork in the storeroom at the back.

'I'm going away for ten days,' I told her.

'Is that wise?'

'Why? What could go wrong?'

When she didn't answer, I said, 'Can you keep an eye on the house for me?'

She gave me a stern look as if I should have known better than to ask. 'I'll keep an eye on it from here, love. Don't ask me to go inside.'

I gave Janak a set of keys. 'Michael will be there for the nights,' I explained. 'If you could drop in during the day, any time you're passing, that would be great. Oh, feel free to use it when you and George want a break from the illegals. Just remember to put the sheets to wash when you're done.'

'Bloody funny,' he said. 'Arsehole!'

That evening I found Janine seated on the bed, paying obeisance to an enormous suitcase open before her.

'Sure you have enough in there? Don't you want to put in the mink coat as well?'

She looked at me seriously. 'You know, I was wondering about that? Doesn't it get cold up in Nuwara Eliya?' Then she realized I was joking and hit me with a pillow. 'We can't all go around looking like tramps.'

'When was the last time you were there?'

'Fifteen years ago? My God, no, eighteen actually!'

'I must have been in my nappies at the time,' I nearly said but shut my mouth in time. I was getting good at avoiding certain pitfalls in the conversation.

I watched her as she packed, the thick black hair gushing down her back like a waterfall, her lips pursed in concentration as she put some clothes into the suitcase, took them out, thought a bit and put them back in again. I had only known her for two brief months, but it felt like forever, as if this was how it had always been. It was her particular brand of genius to make you feel so comfortable, natural, so at home; to make you feel that you were all that mattered, that she and you were the only people left in the world. She did this by clearing her mind of anything else that might take away her concentration. I realize now that this special gift—God-given you might say—is granted only to the very few.

I sat down to my perennial boeuf bourguignon and bottle of red, and was swept away in that easy sense of well-being—a willing passenger in that powerful train of thought, pulling me inexorably on to who-knew-what destination.

*

'Here's fifty pounds, Christmas bonus,' I said to Michael. 'My friend Janak—remember him from the other night? Rivers of blood?—has a key too. He'll drop in during the day.'

'How long are you away for?'

'Ten days. Doing anything special for Christmas Day, Michael? Going to your brothers'?'

But I already knew the answer to that one. Michael smiled condescendingly, as if I was a little simple-minded or something.

'Try not to drink it all,' I said by way of goodbye.

'Can't promise,' he replied.

*

'Now remember,' Janine says on the way to the airport. 'If there's anyone we know on the flight, we only just met, right? Complete coincidence.'

'Why? Why can't we say we're travelling together as friends, or colleagues?'

'You little fool,' she murmurs, fondly mussing up my hair.

We fall at the first fence, of course, at the check-in counter itself.

'Excuse me, excuse me!' I hear someone breathlessly at the back, pushing her way to the front of the queue in the classic Sri Lankan style. 'I'm with them, let me through!'

'Janine! Daaarling!'

'Hello Desiree,' says Janine with lukewarm enthusiasm.

'After *aeons*!'

Does anyone still say 'aeons'? Apparently this woman does, small and solidly built, with flashing coal-black eyes of pure liquid malice.

'And who is this *splendid* young man?'

'This is Sanjay,' Janine says through half-closed eyes, as if she has already been beaten into submission by this other woman. Which, in effect, she has.

'I'm with them,' she says imperiously to the harassed-looking Air Lanka official behind the counter. 'Make sure you put me *right* next to them.'

With some smart footwork we manage to lose her at the duty-free. I would love to buy the Satellites some perfume and a bottle of sweet Martini, their tipple of choice on those long afternoons around the transistor radio. Then I remember that I will not be seeing them. I feel as if I have just stabbed myself in the heart with a kitchen knife. *This is your adult life now, a life of choices. Nobody is forcing you to be disloyal. You're not seeing the Satellites because you have chosen not to see them.* Suddenly, helplessly, I look around for my father to tell me what to do. Of course he is not there, is he! Bloody ghosts. Slippery as spaghetti. All over the plate, never on the end of your fork.

'Exactly who's who did you say you were?' Desiree asks me when we are reunited on the plane after many little squeals of pleasure (on her part), in seats uncomfortably close to each other.

'I didn't.'

'He's Louis' son,' Janine says in that same resigned voice. I have never seen her so despondent, so negative.

'Louis? *Louis!* Oh, good God, the divorce that got away!'

What does she mean by that? I don't want to know. There is too much poison in this woman's words.

'Desiree is Colombo's most eminent divorce lawyer,' Janine explains. 'You are nobody till you have been divorced by her.'

Desiree titters with pleasure. 'When I think of the number of grown men I have reduced to perfect tears in court . . .' She turns to Janine. 'That's why I never took you on, dear. There was never any fight in you, was there. You gave up too easily.'

Curiouser and curiouser. I listen avidly. This doesn't seem to be the Janine I know at all.

'I didn't want Ivor or his money. I wanted my freedom at any cost. I wanted to leave that awful life behind and come to England.'

'I could have got you millions,' Desiree says wistfully. There is a reverential pause while she holds up this sacrament, golden and glittering, to the sound of altar boys' bells. 'But you did all right for yourself, didn't you? Still working—'

'I gave all that up years ago, believe me,' Janine cuts in firmly.

'Yes I can see that,' Desiree says, looking at me sharply. 'It doesn't get any easier as you get older, you know. I can see you're *quite* retired.'

'I have a bit of a headache, Desiree. I think I'll try to get some sleep.' Janine turns towards me (she's seated in the middle), signalling that the conversation is at end. 'Don't wake me when lunch comes around, please.'

I long to hold her hand under the blanket, to comfort her after this merciless verbal assault, but I desist. I feel those coal-black eyes on me—missing nothing, recording everything.

'You coward,' I say to myself, since my father is not there any more to say it.

22

Though it is still early morning, I am touched by that moist kiss of warmth, the merest breath on the face, warning me of the searing heat to come. The soft-as-cloth colours of dawn—cashmere grey and velvet rose and the palest blue shot silk—are already steeped in yellow, as if a careless sun god had spilt a pot of tea over them at breakfast.

I have been away barely three months but I find I hardly recognize anything. Or rather, I recognize it as one might an old photograph, conceding to the accuracy of its representation, unwilling to subscribe to the truth it suggests. The scenes are unquestionably the same—your beloved prosaic mind tells you that—yet it is a struggle to drive your heart to that same point of agreement. Everything is different, you know not why. Finally you realize that the only way you will come to accept the validity of this new-old look is to take a leap of faith, which you do, grumbling all the while that it is likely that you have been conned.

How is it possible that I have changed so much, let go of so much in so short a span of time? Because what else could justify so dramatic a change of perspective?

The mischief in Janine's eyes is back. We have successfully managed to shake Desiree off, refusing her fiendishly kind offer of a lift into Colombo—'I'll drop you wherever you want (just so long as I know where you're staying, so I can tell fifty of my closest friends).'

Colombo at this time has two five-star hotels to speak of: the InterContinental (or Intercon, as it is fondly known) and the Oberoi. We roll into the Intercon and I am struck anew by the lapidary beauty of Janine's features, now lit from below by the shimmering seaside light, a queen stepping superbly out of a rickety red Japanese van. I am immensely proud to have her on my arm as I lead her into the lobby. What does not escape my attention, though, is that particular look we get from everyone—doorman, bellboys, receptionist—you might even call it the 'Desiree look'. Perhaps I should be angry, even ashamed, at this frank and prurient stare: one that assesses with low cunning the sexual, financial and moral implications of this unlikely and esoteric partnership. In some perverse way it has the reverse effect: I am extremely proud that for the first time in my life I have a woman on my arm, that the whole world considers us an item, an indivisible whole. The open mouths only signify that I have passed some obscure manhood test of theirs. I am acutely conscious of the fact that it was a boy who left the country; a man who is returning.

'I have assigned a twin room,' says the receptionist suavely, 'for you and your mother.'

There is a second's pause as the sentence hangs in the air. And then Janine begins to laugh—high notes, low notes, all notes—till the tears begin to run down her face.

'*Mother*?' she hoots. 'This is my boyfriend. Understand? So we need a *double* bed.' She puts her arm around my shoulders to emphasize the point. 'Have *you* ever had a boyfriend? You certainly look as if you could do with one. Shall I arrange one? Shall I?'

I ought to be embarrassed at the sharpness of Janine's pushback; instead, I am proud that she is holding her head high. This may be the first time someone has made that comment. It certainly won't be the last.

I hustle her away from the counter as soon as I can, up to our room overlooking the Indian Ocean. As soon as the bellboy is gone she pulls me on to the bed. 'Our first tropical fuck,' she says, her eyes dancing with slivers of ocean light in them, her hair spread out beneath her in a fan like the giant black feathers of some monsoon bird of prey. 'If only Desiree could see us now!'

*

I have never stayed in a hotel before, let alone a five-star one—mine was never that sort of childhood—yet I seem to be treating all this with the jaded insouciance of the world-weary traveller. I find that I have unexpectedly acquired the condescending eye of so many Sri Lankan expatriates returning home: superior and patronizing, and oh-so benevolent.

But for Janine everything is on point, even if the reality is as haphazard and makeshift as a teenage weekend camping trip. When the AC packs up, I am the one who gets upset. She takes it in her stride—'This is Sri Lanka, what did you expect?'—sweet-talking the receptionist (he who needed the boyfriend) into sending a technician during siesta hour, when all of Sri Lanka is napping, and then tipping him handsomely even though it is part of his job. She puts me to shame with her practical third-world savvy. It is as if she never left. But she has not been back in eighteen years. I am the one who left only three months ago: the traitor who has already crossed over, viewing his country from the superior vantage point of the opposite bank. Though I do not voice it aloud, I am ashamed. I need my father—or the Satellites at least—to cut me down to size, bring me down a notch or two.

'Think I'll take a walk down to Clifford Road this afternoon,' I say. 'See how the old home is. I won't go in, of course.'

She looks worried for a moment. 'Don't let them catch you. It'll be the end of our holiday.'

Home is twenty minutes away on foot, but I must have forgotten that a twenty-minute walk in the heat and humidity is like two hours elsewhere. It is late afternoon. The yellow light has matured to shades of copper and bronze and in the shadows, black iron; coating even the shoddiest building with an antique patina, a burnished air of auction-house mystery. I am walking fast to shake off prospective touts. *How do they know I am a returnee? Three months ago I was a native.* Then I look down and realize why. I am in a pair of shorts Janine bought me. In 1980s Colombo no one walks around in shorts, not in public anyway: it is a crime against decency and humanity. Had my father been around he would have been the first to point this out. 'With legs like yours, Big Feller, you can't afford to take chances.' I walk on, walk fast.

I turn inland at Colpetty Junction, where the wrought iron-and-glass vegetable market of my childhood has been replaced by a brutalist concrete structure, not unlike my own home but uglier—if that were possible. On the opposite side of the road they are building Liberty Plaza, Sri Lanka's first shopping mall. In the coming days I will hear people talk of this iconic landmark with reverence and adoration. It will, of course, rival the Eiffel Tower in Paris and the Colosseum in Rome. It will be up there with the best, establishing Sri Lanka's pre-eminence as one of the great architectural playgrounds of the world.

Down Green Path and on to Clifford Road, where the 1950s still reign supreme. Is this how I remember it? Surely it looks different now in this metallic evening light? The fact is, for the past ten years I must have walked the length of this road every day and not noticed it. Going abroad has had this one beneficial effect: your mind has replaced the over-observed familiarity of the old with a fresh and pleasing new ignorance; you are tasting mutton dressed as lamb, and it is delicious.

The lights are on and I hear the drone of the radio. It is the day before Christmas Eve. No doubt they are all in there wrapping Louis' presents, decorating Louis' tree.

Just then, somebody taps me on the shoulder and I whip around into a cloud of eau-de-cologne—4711.

'I popped out to get some ribbons,' Rani explains. Then she realizes whom she is talking to and there is alarm on her face. She claps a handful of ribbons to her mouth. 'Big Feller!' she says in horror. 'But you're in the UK?'

'Yes, of course! I mean, *no, of course not*!'

She nods wisely. 'You're a ghost then?'

I shake my head. 'I leave that side of things to my father.'

'So?' She is silent, puzzled. Rani was never the brightest bulb in the chandelier, my father would have said. (But then he said this of every Satellite, he was a fair man.) A moment later, realization dawns, flooding her face with an other-worldly, almost spiritual wisdom. She leans close, dropping her voice in case anyone should hear us on this deserted Colpetty street at dusk. 'You're with *him*, aren't you?

'Him?'

'Your special friend? Myrna told us *all* about *him*.'

'What? Oh, yes, him. That's right, *him*. Please don't breathe a word about this to anybody, okay? It's our little secret.'

She looks to the right and left to ensure nobody is listening. 'Of course. Our little secret,' she repeats. 'I'd better go, they'll be waiting for the ribbons.'

'You didn't see me, right?'

'Didn't I?' She looks uncertain for a moment. Then she remembers. 'Of course not.'

It is as if somebody has unscrewed a bottle of happiness and poured it all over me, soaking me thoroughly. The Cult of Louis is alive and well and flourishing in Colpetty. It is running on and on with a life of its own. Neither my father's presence nor mine is necessary for its survival. They are all in there, conducting board meetings and passing resolutions. Minutes are faultlessly recorded, accounts hotly contested. Charitable works are undertaken. And every few minutes someone interjects: 'But that is not how Louis would have wanted it!' or 'I should know. This is what Louis *personally* told *me*.' It is the modern-day equivalent of saying 'Hallelujah!' or 'Amen' in church.

23

The next few days—had I but known it at the time—were probably the happiest of my life. It was almost axiomatic though that I would not realize their worth till they were gone. You only judge the quality of your life in retrospect, needing the wisdom of hindsight to assign comparative value. By then it is too damned late, because the days have slipped through your fingers. All you have left are memories, which you may tell over and over like the beads of an old woman's rosary, but they are only beads after all.

In those days before mobiles and social media, we had no one but ourselves to fall back on; no work to interrupt, no bills to pay, no food to cook. Just eat, fuck, sleep, in no particular order, at no particular time. Downstairs they were going overboard with the Christmas thing—jolly brown Santas singing painfully high-pitched carols in the lobby; an enormous plastic tree all covered in cotton-wool snow; empty boxes at its base cunningly wrapped up in shiny paper.

There was a Christmas Eve dance in the banquet hall. They had taken great care to draw the curtains over the spectacular ocean view, because it is very well known in five-star hotels that Christmas is for reindeers and snow, not for tropical fishing boats lit by kerosene lanterns bobbing up and down on velvet-black seas.

*

Janine and I are seated at a table for ten, eight strangers and us two, behind a forest of tinsel and crêpe paper and glassware. There is an enforced air of jollity, as at a sixth-form dance or some sophisticated mass blind date.

'So, what do you do?', 'What line of work are you in?', 'What part of Sri Lanka are you originally from? And where do you live now?' The questions are the same at every table. This is that time of year when Lankan returnees come home to roost—for that brief week between Christmas and New Year. I realize that most of the people in the room are in the same position as us. They have relations in the hinterland, distant aunts, uncles, cousins. They have set aside a day or two for duty: the statutory well bath and crab curry in Jaffna, the visit to the creaky old *walauwa* home in Kandy, the almsgiving for the dead ancestor in Galle.

For the rest of the time they prefer the comfort of strangers, other returnees like themselves—Sri Lankan, yet not—at sea in a country in which they'll never feel fully at home again, though they might return year after year, often against their better judgement. That night I see myself very plainly within this bigger picture, the way a drunk sometimes attains absolute clarity deep into his cups. I swear to myself that I will never be like them: I will return to settle before it is too late. Though I don't say it, I pray that Janine will return with me. So what if we are ostracized by society? Society can go screw itself. We will have each other.

My neighbour to the right, a techie from Seattle, leans over with the bottle of wine. 'Would your mom like a refill?'

'I'm sure she would,' I say boldly, handing him her glass.

Bring it on, world! Do your worst. I am more than equal to anything you have to throw at me!

*

'Don't you want to go anywhere at all, you lazy beast?' she asks.

'Frankly, no.' It is Christmas Day and we are in bed. We have hardly stirred from the hotel since we got here. There is only the faintest moral compulsion, like a weak earache, telling us we need to go somewhere, do the touristy thing. Back in London before we flew, the talk was all of Kandy or Galle or Sigiriya. Now that we are here, all we want to do is lie in this bed and watch the undulations on the ceiling—like lying at the bottom of a shallow sea and looking at the lazy sun through seawater. With room service, of course.

I reach under the bed. 'This is for you. Merry Christmas!'

She unwraps it. 'You dirty boy! You think I can wear this? I'm a respectable married woman.'

'No, you're not. I wouldn't be with you if you were.'

In return, she presents me with a small box. A thin gold chain, which she puts around my neck.

'I'm not used to wearing chains. I'm sure to lose it.'

'You'd bloody better not. Just make sure you never take it off.'

For Christmas lunch the hotel has decided to empty its freezers. Frozen turkey, frozen sprouts, frozen peas, frozen chestnut stuffing. The dining room reverberates to the sounds of clashing cutlery: all the ersatz good cheer and overblown bonhomie of fellow expats. I am a little perturbed to find that there is no yellow rice and chicken curry on the menu. Like the fishing boats, they don't seem to feature in this frozen five-star Christmas.

And then my blood freezes too. I see approaching that terrifyingly familiar line of un-five-star footwear—scuffed court shoes, leather sandals, Bata slippers. It is too late to make a run for it. The Satellites are upon us, grim-faced and ashen, a small battalion armed for conflict.

'Desiree called to say you were in town.'

'It took *ages* to figure out where you were, which hotel you were in.'

'Phyllis had to phone around. Use all her charm.'

'Were you planning to go away without seeing us at all? Big Feller, how *could* you!'

Janine looks up from her lunch. 'Because of me, maybe?' She laughs scornfully.

This is entirely the wrong thing to say. Any sympathy the Satellites might have had for this shamelessly guilty couple, found *in flagrante delicto*, vanishes instantly. Forgiveness, if there had ever been a promise of it, is now a thing of the past.

Myrna faces Janine squarely, in battle stance. 'Shut up, you brazen hussy! You witch!' she spits out. She is breathing loudly, her chest rising and falling with the effort of this charge. I have never seen her so overwrought, heard her so spiteful. I realize what it must have taken for her to say this, what emotional cost.

'Brazen? I like that. *Brazen.*' Janine laughs again, shaking her head at some private joke too absurd to share. She goes back to her lunch disdainfully.

Myrna turns to me. 'I brought you up. I am a *mother* to you.'

The Seattle techie is following this shouting match with great interest. I know what he is thinking: *How many mothers does this lucky guy have?*

I stand up. 'Myrna, Phyllis, Kamala, Rani. I'm only hiding here because I knew you wouldn't approve.' To emphasize my point, I go and stand behind Janine's chair, putting my hands on her shoulders. Even at this gravest of moments I am aware of the thick black hair erupting through my fingers, an unseasonable tropical crop. 'Get this. We're together. Understood?'

The Satellites stand open-mouthed and silent, like figures in a wax museum. For that matter the entire dining room is open-mouthed and silent. It is like Madame Tussauds in there. The Tussauds InterContinental.

'If you're not going to join us, leave us to enjoy our lunch,' Janine says loudly for the benefit of the whole dining room.

The Satellites turn, defeated, like a row of surrendering soldiers. They begin to march out. I run after them. 'Myrna, please. I'll come and see you. Promise.'

'Don't you dare!' she says fiercely. 'After all that we have done for you!' The tears in her eyes are breaking my heart; at the same time they are reaffirming my convictions. It is Janine I want. Unquestionably. Absolutely.

Myrna dabs her eyes with a tissue. 'My God, where did we go wrong? We did so much for you.'

I hang my head in shame. I know too well the truth of what she is saying.

'What would Louis say?'

'Actually, Louis fully approves. You should hear him on the subject,' I want to reply. But I can't. It would kill them, push them over the edge entirely.

'You'll live to regret this. One day, you'll be sorry. And we won't be there to help you.'

Rani has the last word. She turns around, breaking formation, and says to me in a hushed whisper: 'Just one thing, Big Feller. It's not that important, really. I just wanted to know. What did you do with your special friend? Where have you hidden *him*? Upstairs?'

I go back into the dining room. All the returnees immediately look away, avoiding eye contact scrupulously. Even Janine does not look up as she calmly continues eating.

*

This episode has left me drained. I am not used to emotional battles, I never was. It was always easier to give in, hug my defeat to myself and carry on. This is the first time I have fought a battle on behalf of someone else and won. Buried somewhere inside that wide bank of exhaustion is a little worm of elation wriggling to get out. It is five in the evening and we have eaten too much. We walk through the crowds on Galle Face Green outside the hotel, through the cacophony of whistles and plastic toy trumpets, men selling lottery tickets through hand-held megaphones and others lighting crackers—all the good-natured roar of a Christmas day in the tropics. We have come to watch the sunset, but there is no sun. It is hidden behind a cloud, blushing with embarrassment at Myrna's outburst.

The surrounding noise means that conversation is almost impossible. A good thing, because there is everything to say and nothing to say, and neither of us has the will to articulate this nothingness. The scene in the dining room painted a line around us, protecting and isolating us at the same time. We have faced the worst, and the worst has backed down. Today is the first day of the armistice and my whole body is glowing with the weariness of the victor.

'Let's come back and settle here,' I say later in bed.

'Here?' Her face registers the hopelessness, the absurdity of my suggestion. 'Maybe when we're old and not much good for anything else?' She does not laugh. I know she is not joking.

'I love you,' I whisper as we drift off to sleep.

'No you don't. It's all in your mind.'

*

In my sleep, I dream of great white sharks swimming in blackened angry water. I am on the seabed, trying to remain inconspicuous. I know it is only a matter of time before they come for me.

Somewhere in the middle of the night, I am woken up by the ringing of a telephone. At this moment I don't know where I am. The curtains aren't closed properly and I notice it is still dark outside, the glimmerings of a fractured moon silvering a sea of ink.

'I am sorry to disturb you at this hour, sir. There is a call for you from London. May I put it through?'

24

For a second I can't place the voice. Then it swims back into my consciousness, gobbling up the last remaining shreds of sleep. It is Janak.

'Thank God you're still up,' he says.

No point telling him I was not actually up, that it was his call that woke me.

'Michael is dead.'

'*What? Michael*?' I sit up. Janine is stirring, her eyelids fluttering open.

'I was away with George these last couple of days. We came back this afternoon. I thought I'd just pop in . . .' His voice chokes. 'Michael was seated at the kitchen table. Dead. And you know what? There was a frying pan on the stove and the gas was still on.'

'Oh my God! Michael?' I can't make sense of what he's trying to tell me. Then I hear a funny echo by my side. It's Janine.

'Michael?' she repeats.

I cup the receiver, turning to her: 'The watcher on the site. *He's dead!*'

'Michael? Mick? Oh my God, Micky?' An eerie keening sound escapes her lips and she rolls from side to side and the bed shakes. I watch with horror. It is as if she is possessed.

'Are you still there?' Janak asks.

'Tell me what I have to do.'

'You need to fly back as soon as you can. The police may want a statement from you.'

I can hear what he is saying but my attention is on what is going on in this room, which has turned into a chamber of horrors. Janine has got out of bed. She's huddled in a corner, squatting. 'Micky!' she is wailing. 'Oh my God, my Micky!'

'I'll call you back as soon as I can,' I say quickly and hang up. I go to Janine and attempt to put my arms around her.

'Go away!' she screams. '*Murderer*. I never wanted him to work for you. He's dead because of you!'

'Janine,' I say desperately. 'You don't even know him.'

'Don't know him?' Her voice is shrill and she's laughing and crying at the same time. Her tear-stained face is twisted in bitterness. 'He's my husband, you fool!'

*

We manage to get seats on next day's flight. Janine's face is carved in stone, a statuesque goddess frozen in life as in death.

'Speak to me!' I say desperately. 'What is going on?'

'You mentioned the name and I realized it was him working for you. I didn't want him to. I knew it would end badly.'

'Why should it matter to you? Your marriage is history. You divorced him a long time ago.'

'Divorced? I'm still married to him.'

'But he means *nothing* to you. You're with me now.'

She says nothing. Her eyes say it all.

'You don't love him!' I say desperately. I am naked now, snatching at any scrap of clothing to cover my humiliation.

'Love? *Love*?' I hear that scornful tone I have come to know so well these last few days. 'What would *you* know about love?'

I am like a cat playing with a dead mouse, trying to make it come alive only so I can kill it again. 'You don't love him. You may have done then. You don't now.'

She puts her hand tentatively on my arm. 'We were married for four years before I threw him out. You don't just fall out of love from one day to the next. It's not like turning off a light switch.'

'Then what were you doing with me these last couple of months? What were you doing in Sri Lanka?'

'This was your idea, not mine.' She gives me a despairing look, as if I could never hope to understand, that these things were beyond my ken; and she is right about that.

'Of course you didn't think to tell me? You pretended you didn't know who he was. You lied to me. You made me the laughing stock of the entire building site!'

'Because I knew how you'd react. Exactly like you're reacting now!' She turns away from me. 'You're giving me a headache. I'm going to sleep now.'

She lapses into a fog-bound, silence-ridden world. We fly through the clouds side by side, together but apart, all the way back.

*

I went back to Tintern Street. It wasn't as if I had much stuff at her flat anyway—it was all in my bag.

'Michael had gone on a drinking binge,' Janak said. 'On the morning of the 23rd, he called his brothers to ask if he could come for Christmas dinner. They said no.'

'The bastards.'

'He was picked up later that day, supposedly for being drunk and disorderly. You know what the sus laws are like around here. The police can pick you up for anything. Even if they don't like the look on your face.'

'And then?'

'They released him next morning after he'd sobered up. Christmas Eve. He must have died some time that day or the next. The empty frying pan was on the stove, the rashers of bacon on the counter. His Christmas lunch. And the fire was still on under the pan when I found him.' Janak shivered. 'He was just seated there, blue in the face. As if he'd seen a ghost or something.'

'But what did he die of?'

Janak shrugged. 'Was he beaten up by the police? Internal haemorrhaging? You know what they're like in Brixton.'

'But he was white, not black.'

'I know. That's the strange part.'

'So there's no autopsy? No official cause of death?'

'It seems they don't even want to interview you.' Janak got up. 'Funeral's tomorrow. They're all expecting you. It's meet-the-Mulrooneys time.'

25

Ted Mulrooney lived in a neat bungalow in Chislehurst. The front garden was well-tended, the paintwork on the house immaculate; a million miles away from Michael's world. I went there with Sean in his shiny chocolate-coloured Volvo. It was just about the oldest, most banged-up car of the many parked outside the house for the funeral.

Mrs Ted opened the door to us, a woman in a stout black dress and iron-grey close-cropped hair. She looked at us doubtfully for a moment. 'You must be Mr Silver? Come in. Welcome to our humble home.'

There was a doormat across the threshold that said 'Welcome.' Also, several cross-stitched samplers on the walls proclaiming 'East or West, Home is Best' and 'Home Sweet Home'.

'A sad business, Mr Silver. Michael was very dear to us as you know. He will be missed.'

'Obviously not dear enough,' Sean muttered as we followed her in. The others were already there. Ernie and Jo, and even Douglas, got up in their Sunday best, wriggling uncomfortably, as if it was their first day in school. At the far end of the room was a table laid with plates and glasses and food: cold roast chicken, carrots and radishes and spring onions, and a glass platter prettily arranged with slices of ham. There were also gherkins and pickled onions, and a jar of Branston Pickle.

'We lead a simple life, Mr Silver. We are extremely simple people.'

'With extremely simple minds,' said Sean under his breath, coughing heavily.

'Shut the fuck up,' I growled.

The Mulrooneys were all seated at the table looking solemn in white shirts. I was thankful I had gone shopping and picked up a thin black tie. In contrast, Sean was in T-shirt and jeans, and I felt the censorious Mulrooney eye fall heavily upon him. Looking around, I was puzzled that Michael would have wanted all this, had actively aspired to it: the 'surbitonization' of his life, Janine might have said.

Just then the doorbell rang and I felt sick in my stomach. I knew who it was: I had only just thought of her after all. I knew how people tended to materialize in front of me the moment I thought of them; my special gift. She was all in black: black boots, slim black trousers cut high on the waist to accentuate her hourglass shape and a bum-freezer jacket also in black, over a white shirt. On her feet were patent leather shoes with impossible heels high as cocktail sticks, more suitable as murder weapons.

'Hah, the black widow,' Ernie said quite loudly, flashing me a covert, cunning look. The others grinned, digging each other in the ribs. I ignored them, thinking to myself: even Ernie knew. I was the only one who didn't, the mug, the one they had all successfully kept out of the loop. It was the shame of it that I couldn't bear, the loss of face. As if they had said: *Sanjay, will you go out into the garden and play like a good child? Excuse us, won't you, while we get on with this little thing called real life?*

She sat down, her eyes grazing over me with barely a flicker of recognition. Then she turned resolutely away to talk to the Mulrooneys. Within minutes she had them in her thrall, this woman with her pretend city sophistication. There was something about this act that angered me, brought out the savage from somewhere inside. 'Don't be fooled,' I wanted to say out loud. 'Just roll her over on to her back and she'll show you a lovely trick or two. I guarantee it.'

I sat there feeling alienated—a comfortable, comforting return to my earlier Sri Lankan life: the outsider in the other room listening to the World Service next door.

The Mulrooneys were talking about the strip farm in Donegal they had left behind, a narrow ribbon of land stretching all the way from the mountains to the sea.

'That's where Michael belonged,' said Ted. 'He should never have left.'

That would have been convenient, I thought. Out of sight, out of mind. No explanations needed to cover up for any embarrassing un-English behaviour.

'He never fitted in,' said Pat's wife, a harassed-looking individual with a whine to her voice. 'Anyone could tell you that.'

I thought to myself: *Is this what they will say of me too if I fall down dead on a London street?* I swore yet again that this would not be me.

The conversation had turned—as sure as the leaves turn red in autumn, Michael would have said—to Buckingham Palace. They were on surer ground now, with Ted's wife leading the way. 'You know we went to see the Changing of the Guard last week? A *fine* body of marching men!' She sighed. Whether for the men or the march I could not tell.

I was waiting for Janine to come out with her own Royal Family stories—it would have rounded out this immigrant love-fest, made my happiness complete—but she was carefully silent on the subject. Then she said musingly: 'You know I very nearly persuaded Michael to go out to Sri Lanka with me to settle down? He chickened out at the last minute.' She laughed.

I felt dizzy. I had offered her the very same thing a couple of days ago and she had thrown it back in my face. It was sticky and close in there with the heat of all this self-righteousness and I found I could not breathe. I opened the French windows and went out into the garden, with its denuded plants, its brown patch of lawn. And there in the middle of the brown patch was my father.

'You!' I exclaimed. 'That's all I need.'

He put up his hand as if to ward off a blow. 'I know what happened. You don't have to tell me.'

'I suppose you're going to take her side,' I said angrily.

'You know she'll take you back? If you ask her nicely.'

'Are you fucking out of your mind?'

'Suit yourself. It's your life. Not mine.' He fell silent. Examining the dead roses, no doubt. This ghost that had never looked at a garden his entire life.

'Not up to much as funerals go, is it, Sanjay?' he said changing the subject. 'You and I, we're experts on the subject, aren't we? *Experts.* So tell me about Sri Lanka. How was Myrna? How was the old bat?'

'I wasn't intending to meet her. She found out.'

'How did she take to your, er, your fiancée?'

'Not well. She called her a brazen hussy.'

My father giggled. Then he looked up. 'Well the brazen hussy is on her way out to speak to you right now.'

'Sanjay!' she called out smiling. 'Come here, I want to talk to you.' The very loudness of her voice, the cheery look on her face made me loathe her even more.

'Can we be friends?'

Friends? How could she even suggest it?

She took my arm. 'This is how life is, Big Feller.' She had never called me Big Feller before. It only added to her insincerity. 'There's no logic to it. This is how I am, how I feel. That's all there is to it.'

And if there's a betrayal or two along the way, I thought bitterly, *who's to blame*?

She stood there proudly, her blazing black luxuriance a taunt to those impoverished wintry surroundings, the bare-boned bushes, the dead ghost.

But I was unmoved. 'Tell me one thing,' I said. 'When Michael asked me for a week's leave that day, after Myrna came to London, was that . . . did he . . .?'

She smiled mischievously, saying nothing. I had all the answer I needed. I felt sick in my stomach. *Who was this woman?*

In fact, had any of it been for real? *Tell me,* I wanted to beg, *tell me that at least some of it was for real. Please tell me that I meant even one tiny little bit to you.* But the same pride that had stopped me from asking about my mother kicked in. I stayed silent.

'I never made any promises to you,' she said cleverly. Oh, the slick casuistry of the lawyer, for whom it is all about the letter and not the spirit! Desiree was wrong about her, I thought. Together they would have made a fine pair, given that first husband a great run for his millions. They would have stripped him of everything he had, like turpentine on varnish.

'If I gave you the wrong impression, I am sorry.'

'Yeah, right.'

'One day, when you're grown up, you'll realize my position.'

'Grown up?' I shouted. 'Grown up?' It was freezing in that garden but I could feel the sweat pouring off my face. In that moment I knew I *had* grown up, that half a lifetime had passed in those few seconds. I would never be the same again no matter what I did: there would always be that faint residue, the slight taint of bitterness at the bottom of that toxic glass; what the world fondly, romantically, mistakenly, calls *experience*.

But right in the middle of all this a disturbing thought struck me: so what if her behaviour didn't fit into the narrow cloistered morality that I had grown up with? Didn't my inability to cope with this betrayal say more about me than her? I was perfectly willing to entertain, true or not, salacious tales of workers' adventures with various girlfriends and mistresses. How was this any different? Why shouldn't a woman act as cavalierly, as dishonestly as any man, and not get away with it? Weren't we all free to fuck whom we chose, when we chose? I wasn't married to her, was I?

Perhaps the fault really was in me. In order to understand her, I needed to understand myself first. I realized in that moment that there was a part of me unknown even to myself, hidden away for too long, which I had to reclaim if I ever hoped to acquire this knowledge. A vital piece of the jigsaw that had rolled away under the sofa, left to be chewed up by the dog.

'I think this is yours,' I said, taking the chain off my neck. She looked at it cursorily, the way a man might. Then she put it away. Business as usual.

'Don't forget that I'm still your agent!' she called out cheerily as I turned away. 'I'll still be selling your flats for you.'

'Right,' I said. 'You do that.'

*

Sean drove me back. My father joined us for the journey, sitting in the back of the car exhaling his ghostly vapours, complaining bitterly about the decline in quality of funerals these days.

'It's a little stuffy in here, isn't it?' Sean said. 'Do you mind putting your window down a little?'

We drove through endless manicured suburbs. After a while I said, 'You knew, didn't you?'

Sean nodded.

'Why didn't you say anything?'

He turned around. 'Look, Ernie wanted to tell you. You know how he is. Loves to be the bearer of bad news. I stopped him.'

'You?'

'I could see you were enjoying yourself. Would've been a shame to put a stop to it.' He grinned, taking great care not to look at me. 'Looked like you needed it. Besides, why should it matter? It's a free world, isn't it?'

And I thought: *How right he is. Why did it matter so much to me?*

We drove in silence for a while. Then I said: 'I'm the idiot here, aren't I? The absolute fucking idiot?'

He didn't say anything, just kept his eyes on the road.

*

Back home, my father sat watching me make a mug of tea in the kitchen. 'I'm sitting in Michael's chair,' he said. 'Poor bastard.'

'Well he's over on your side now, isn't he?'

'How much longer do you have in this house?'

'Another few weeks. I move to the new site as soon as the ground floor's sold.'

'In the meantime, go away.'

'Go away? Why would I go away? I only just came back.'

'I think they got the wrong man,' he said softly.

'*They?*' I felt the hairs rise on my arm.

'You'll be safe once you're in the new place,' he whispered. 'If you can be away for the next two weeks, it'll be good.'

Had he been right all along? Was there really something in this house that was beyond the normal, beyond the rational? Then an even more horrifying thought struck me. 'Did *you* have anything to do with all this?'

'Of course not,' he said quickly. But he looked guilty as hell. He was such a humbug that you never knew whether to believe him or not. His life-long motto had always been: why tell the truth when a fib will do?

'Were you, in some mad way, trying to get rid of Michael to clear the way for Janine and me? Is that why you want me to go back to her?'

'You know you should be writing novels? You have such fanciful ideas?

'Big Feller, please,' he continued after a while. 'You have to believe me. I'm only here because you need me. There's a necessity for my presence.'

'Yeah, right. I'm finally making a go of things, selling these flats, and you can't bear to be out of the picture. You want the credit, that's the real reason you're here.'

'Sanjay! How can you say that? Your success is a *direct* result of the way I brought you up. Isn't that credit enough? What more would I want?'

'Always ends up having to be about you, doesn't it?' I said bitterly.

'As long as I'm here, you're safe. You don't have to worry, nothing will touch you. You have my word.'

Was he lying? The way an adult might lie to comfort a child? (Go to sleep, darling, Daddy will protect you from the dragons!) Then again, was I being hard on him? Perhaps he was telling the truth after all?

Then something really strange happened. Something inside me turned, suddenly, the way a swimmer flips at the end of the pool in readiness for the next length, and I knew with absolute conviction he was telling the truth: he was here for no other reason than to keep me out of harm's way. In spite of my cynicism and all his shiftiness, evergreen and unkillable, I couldn't shake off this intuition. I had a sudden urge then—irrational and absurd—to thank him, shake his hand, hug him close, do all those things a normal son might do to a normal father, things I had never dreamt of doing while he was still alive. But now, when I wanted to, I found I physically couldn't. He was only a column of cold, cold air.

So instead I did what I had always done. I took one last dig. 'It so happens,' I said, 'I do have somewhere to go to. Only you're not going to like it and it serves you bloody well right!'

PART IV

26

Paddington Station looks like the inside of a morgue in the curious grey half-light, a light of bleached bones and drained carcasses; the colour of the death you must leave behind in order to find new life.

'It's a long journey,' the man behind the ticket counter says doubtfully. 'You have to get down at Exeter St David's and walk to St David's Station. Then get down at Church and walk another quarter of a mile. Over four hours of travel time.'

'Never mind,' I say. 'I have all the time in the world. A few weeks in fact.'

On the train I take out the black-and-white photo with the crinkled edges. Even though it is winter, I can smell the honeysuckle. It's been almost fifty years. The house may not even be there. It may be sold, its occupants dispersed. Only one way to find out. There is still the faintest fleeting chance that the missing piece of the jigsaw is here—washed up in this lonely part of Devon on the edge of Dartmoor—

in a little village with the lovely name of Zeal Monachorum.

*

The pre-fab cabin interior smelt like an ashtray. 'Where to?' asked the man at the switchboard.

'Do you know of a house around here called Alleyn Court?'

He looked at me doubtfully. 'Come visiting, have you?'

I didn't know what he meant. He spoke into his headset and a minicab from the rank outside slid silently up. I got in. We drove in silence down roads one-car-wide, lined with high hedges. There were lay-bys every hundred yards, so that if you met oncoming traffic one of you had to reverse. A system that would never have worked with Sri Lankan drivers: those Devon country lanes would have been clogged with cars, all at permanent stand-off with each other.

The driver looked at me in the rear-view mirror. 'What brings you to Alleyn Court?'

'There's a family I used to know who lived there.'

'What? The Gaisfords? All gone, mate, all gone. There was a brother and sister, I remember. Sold up and went to the States I think. Still want to go?'

'Why not,' I said bleakly.

We took an unmarked turn and bumped for a while down a rutted red road. If I was expecting a grand country house with sweeping vistas, I was going to be disappointed. Coming to a stop at a wide gate with horizontal iron bars which the driver opened, we bumped slowly over a cattle grid, then down a curving drive, arriving finally at a long low house—unplanned, organic, ancient: a house exuding the sort of harmony you can only attain through half a millennium of existence. A board planted in front read: 'Alleyn Court Care Home.'

*

I paid off the driver. 'You want me to wait?' he asked.

I shook my head. 'I may be a while.'

He gave me a card with a number to call for the return journey and drove off, with a cheerful screech of gravel that left me feeling even more bereft. I pushed open the front door and went inside.

A woman rose from a rather smart desk positioned at the front of a black-and-white tessellated hallway hung with mirrors. 'Sister Edey,' she said. 'Can I help you?'

'I'm not sure,' I replied hesitantly. 'I used to know the people who lived here, the Gaisfords. Do you think I might have a look around?'

'You've come to see *Domenica!*' she said. 'Wonderful! She gets so few visitors.'

'*Domenica?*'

My legs began to give way and I had to lean against the desk. I found my fingertips had turned to ice. I rubbed them together, feeling the moisture that had inexplicably appeared on them.

'I don't recall seeing you here before. Are you a friend?'

I was using all the muscles of my diaphragm to control my breath. I pumped and pumped silently, in-out-in-out, while she watched me curiously. I was running. That final mile around the park.

'Are you all right? Can I get you a glass of water?'

I shook my head. *Remember, none of this can touch you now. Your mind is floating, far above and free. It has nothing to do with this world below.*

'Are you a friend?' she asked again.

'I suppose you could say that. Tell me . . . how long has she been living here?'

Sister Edey paused for a moment. 'Let's see. I've been here a good thirteen, no, fourteen years. She arrived just before me, so fifteen?'

I thought of all those years. All those years missing from the life I might have had.

'A brave woman, that. Just checked herself in when she realized her condition. No other family, you see. Only this brother. So she came right back here.'

No other family? What about me? I wanted to shout. *Don't I count?*

I wanted to throw chairs at the pier glasses, break the furniture, smash all the windows of that lovely hall. I wanted to howl so loud the sound would carry to the edges of Dartmoor and beyond. I wanted to kill them all, because they had killed me. But in the space of those few minutes I calmed down. *What was the point?* There it was again, above and all around: the blank page of that lovely, empty, unreadable sky.

It was lucky that I had found her even this late. But there was one word in there that worried me. 'You said "condition"?'

'Early onset.' She smiled. 'Of course it helped that her brother owned this pile. You know he turned it into a nursing home just so she could be happy these last years of her life? Lives in the States now, though he's still our landlord. But why am I telling you this? You know it already. You're a *friend*!'

All I could think was, fifteen years. *Fifteen, fucking, fucking years.*

She led me up the broad wooden staircase to the first floor, to one of the best rooms in the house, perhaps the very same one I had not been allowed to sleep in all those years ago. 'Before you go in, I must warn you. She will keep repeating herself. Be patient and try not to contradict, it'll only upset her. Best to go along with whatever she says.' She knocked once and threw open the door. 'Visitor for you, Domenica,' she called out cheerfully.

'I'll leave you then, shall I?' Sister Edey said to me quietly and closed the door on us.

Seated in the bow window, against the backdrop of a wintry Devon sky, was a small pink woman with curly hair soft as candyfloss. I reflected sadly: *There is absolutely nothing of her in me, nor me in her*. She was just another little old English lady you might pass on the High Street without a second glance.

'Finally! I thought you were never coming!' she said. 'But where's the ladder? How do you think you're going to fix the curtain without a ladder?'

'I forgot. I'm sorry.'

'Every morning the sunlight streams in through that gap there, right there at the top,' she gestured with her long tapered fingers—fingers that I recognized with a shock because they were my own too. 'I've been telling them for years. You think they'll listen to an old woman?'

She leant forward conspiratorially. 'Shall I let you in on a little secret? All this belongs to me!'

'No, really?'

'Yes! All of it. And they're trying to take it off me. Can you believe it?'

'Wicked, wicked world,' I murmured. I meant it.

'But let's talk about you. What part of the world are *you* from?'

'Sri Lanka,' I said hesitantly, not knowing how much she would remember.

'Don't think I know where that is.' She shook her head. 'So difficult . . . all these new countries nowadays!' she laughed and I was glad because wherever she was, I knew it was a happy place. 'Do you know, I knew a chap from *Ceylon* once?'

'Did you?' I asked, my interest quickening.

'Delightful. Delightful old rogue.'

I grinned happily. 'You can say that again.'

I stayed another half hour listening to her patter, comforting as rain on an old tiled roof. As rain on barren land after fifteen parched years, you might say. I promised myself that I would come every day while I was here, as often as I could thereafter.

'Make sure you bring the ladder next time,' she said imperiously as I got up to go. 'You people, you're just the best, aren't you?' She chuckled confidentially. 'Us Brits, we're hopeless. *Hopeless*.'

Sister Edey called up the taxi. While we waited, I forced myself to ask the question I most feared.

'How long?'

She frowned. 'It's difficult with early onset. It's a rare condition you know? Ten years?'

'But—'

'I know.' She smiled gently. 'Not long now.'

'Think I'll walk a bit outside while I wait,' I said. 'If you don't mind.'

Of course I could follow the intellectual justification for her actions. The justification that so many suicides used, and believers of euthanasia: to spare other people their sadness, their pain. Yet, at its deepest level, it was the most selfish of actions, one that reckoned without the heart. *Didn't I have the right to suffer on her behalf? Who was she to ration my grief? Does the mother who gives life to her son have the right to take it away too?* Because when you thought about it, that was exactly what she had done: even if she hadn't physically taken my life, she had both comprehensively and effectively killed off any life I might have had as her son. *And where did all of this leave my father? How complicit was he in these plans?* Her actions might explain his lifetime of silence: *why was he not man enough to rise above them?* As for the charade of that fictitious grave at Bullers Road Cemetery—it was both manipulative and cruel to subject a child to that.

I shook my head in despair. It was too late now. The time for recriminations was long gone. You cannot replace the accretions of fifteen lost years. The train had long since pulled out of the station: all I had now was the presence of its absence, the thin scent of metal bitter and sharp, hanging uncertain in the wintry air. To visit my mother now was to visit a stranger; a charitable act at best.

One thought did occur to me though. All those roads I might or might not have taken throughout my entire life—all had beckoned me to this very spot, to this precise moment in time. All those events—my father's cancer, my decision to stay on in England till I was thirty, even Janine—were only an integral part of this richer, grander, more complex design. My job perhaps was simply to submit to the will of this design with the best grace I could muster.

As I tramped about in that cold, the frozen gravel crunching underfoot, I longed to be back in London. I could kill that bloody ghost. He had a lot of explaining to do.

27

'How could you let her go? Why didn't you stop her? Why?'

My father and I were in the kitchen, he in Michael's chair, and I in my usual place by the sink.

'Oh, don't be a child, Sanjay. She was more stubborn even than you. I couldn't have stopped her if I tried.'

'But you didn't try! That's the whole point. You just stood by and watched her go.'

'She knew England was the best place for her. In her condition.'

'But you could have told me. You hid it from me!' The tears were running down my face. I couldn't stop them.

'Sanjay, listen to me. Just imagine if you knew? You would have wanted to join her.' My father shook his head. 'I wasn't having any of that. She could barely manage on her own. She couldn't have managed a child as well. Not over there. Not in her condition.'

I looked at him scornfully. 'It didn't occur to you that you could have gone with her? Helped her out? Oh, no. Much easier to sit at home in comfort, doing sod all!'

'Comfort? Ha! Is that what you call it?' My father snorted. 'No, Sanjay, I couldn't imagine any sort of life over there. Eating parippu soup heated over the hotplate in some bed-sit. Freezing because we couldn't afford the coins for the meter.' He shivered. It made me think of Janak around the corner. 'Besides, she didn't want me there.'

'*That's because you didn't love her!*'

'Love? What do you know about love, Sanjay? Of course I loved her. I just didn't *like* her. She was impossible in so many ways.' My father was lost in thought for a moment.

'I think you'll come to realize, Sanjay, that it's a little too much to ask for in life. To find both love and like in the same equation.'

*

So, this then is the incredible story of my parents. A father who continues to plague me from beyond the grave, attempting to manipulate my every action, attempting perhaps to live vicariously through me the life he never had—though he might try to tell you otherwise. And a mother who was dead to me long before she really died, cut out of my life the way they cut the tonsils from a child's throat supposedly for his own good, or the claws off a Manhattan cat so it won't ruin the carpets in the apartment.

She died six months later. When she did I found, unaccountably, I was too busy to attend the funeral. I had just bought an old house on Rita Road, Vauxhall, opposite the malt vinegar factory. Every time the wind blew in our direction it brought with it that acetic smell—sour and sad as an alcoholic's breath. That was funeral enough for me.

Was this the real reason I didn't attend, was I really that busy? Was it too traumatic for me to handle? One death so close upon another? But it seemed to me I had been born, bred and raised on a diet of grief. It was nothing new, nothing unexpected. So it couldn't have been that. Was there another reason then? Some little sediment of spite, perhaps, stirred up from the bottom of the coffee cup after all this time? Fifteen years ago, she had wilfully and willingly deconstructed me, her son, so I would become no more to her than a faraway figment of her imagination. Perhaps it was payback time: time for me to make her a figment of mine. She had been dead to me these fifteen long years. That extra day, the day of her actual death, wasn't going to make any difference. Or so I reasoned. In fact, when I think back to my actions now, all I feel is shame, shame that will live with me for as long as I live.

It is a terrible thing to take revenge upon the dead. But before you judge me, dear reader, for this heinous act of an ungrateful son, ask yourself this one question: Who abandoned whom, exactly, in this shabby little tale?

As for my father, that is a whole other story. *Who was this ghost? Was he for real? Did I exhume and reconstruct a dead man in my imagination just because I had some urgent need to?*

I don't really know the answer to these questions. All I know is that under his tutelage, in the eight years of the Thatcher '80s left to me, I went on to develop and sell eighty-four flats in south London, holding the freeholds to them all till the bitter end, when I cashed in my chips and returned to Sri Lanka. But that is an entirely different story, one that has no place in the pages of this book.

'Keep it small,' my father once warned me. 'Always be in control. Never forget who you are, a small-time Asian builder in a world of big boys.'

Gee, thanks, Dad! I thought back then. Looking back, those were the soundest words of advice anyone ever gave me.

28

After my father's funeral, goaded on by the Satellites into what seemed then a highly uncharacteristic course of action—with my father gone it was unnecessary to escape Sri Lanka, to go anywhere at all—I visited Myrna's travel agent, an old man for whom customers were apparently a painful inconvenience.

'What do you want to go to Italy for?' he snapped.

'My father passed away two weeks ago. It was a place he always wanted to visit.' I shifted uncomfortably in the sweat-inducing orange plastic chair. 'I kind of feel I owe it to him.'

'You'll need a visa,' he said disapprovingly.

I didn't want to point out that his job as a travel agent was to book my flight, not question my choice of destination. I took out my passport and showed him the bright, wavy blue certificate of patriality that the UK High Commission had stamped on it two days ago. 'I'm told that with this, the Italian visa should not present a problem.'

He took the passport to examine it, making a little whistling noise through his teeth, as if a kettle was boiling. I almost said 'milk and two sugars please'. He carefully went through the other pages, all of which were blank. It was highly irregular. Britain was the holy grail of all asylum and jobseekers, adventurers and chancers. You only went to France or Italy or elsewhere (in strict descending order, with Albania and Mongolia somewhere near the bottom), if you couldn't get into the UK.

Why on earth would you want to go through purgatory when there was a direct flight to heaven?

*

I got off the plane in Rome, stashed my cardboard suitcase and clinking-clanking holdall in the left luggage, and took the train to Arezzo. The bus stand was just outside the railway station, a wide low Mussolini-style piazza with the old town stretching up into the hills in front. It was late September and the heat rose from the tarmac in little swirls and eddies, like so many hungry colourless worms. I had to wait over an hour; they said I was lucky to get a bus.

You approach Anghiari through a straight Roman road that dips and rises through the shimmering stillness, then loops through the town, twisting back on itself like a Möbius strip. It was two-thirty in the afternoon in the dog days of summer, that last violent spate of heat before autumn sets in, moist and purple, to douse the flames for another year.

'Nnghri,' he had said, his last words to me. Anghiari. *Had he ever been here, to talk so knowledgeably of it? Had he come here with my mother at some unknown time in the past?*

I walked through those deserted streets and alleys, and everywhere I expected to see him—peeping through a green louvred door here, leaning over the rails of a balcony there; or simply seated on those cool stone steps leading to the door under that arch. And I felt rather than saw the path of my life to come—a series of rooms opening endlessly, silently, one into another, all empty—a journey of heart-stopping loneliness.

Finally I found myself back in the square, at a group of eight trestle tables arranged under an awning that offered scant shade, occupied by a single cat. There was a radio on, chattering ceaselessly in Italian with the spurious good humour of the professional DJ. Only the cat was listening; then it leapt lightly down to the ground and disappeared.

I looked up at the blank page of that great unreadable sky, then down at the valley spread below. It was seared yellow and the little cars on the Roman road rose and fell like metallic beads of mercury in a thermometer. A young girl—she couldn't have been more than fourteen—came out and explained that the kitchen was closed, but she would be happy to get me a cool drink, or a coffee perhaps? I waved my hand to say it didn't matter.

I thought of my father, how I had loathed him in life, how I longed for him in death: and sitting here in this strange country, entirely removed from my existence, I could see this existence, spread out in its entirety across the valley below, beginning to end, like a frayed yellow tablecloth.

Little did I know then what I know now, that this was not the end at all but the beginning. That our lives—my father's and mine—were like that Möbius strip. You took a pair of scissors and cut it carefully down the middle, dividing it in two to achieve that longed-for separation; only to find you had ended up with two loops inextricably intertwined, like the links of a chain. A mathematical miracle to none but a fool like yourself.

The young girl leant over, concerned. '*Ma signore, sta piangendo?* Hey mister, are you crying?'

I shook my head. 'It must be the wind in my eyes,' I said.

Acknowledgements

I am hugely indebted to my editors—Tarini Uppal and Aslesha Kadian—and to Mrinali Thalgodapitiya, for their invaluable comments on this manuscript; and as ever to Mita Kapur, my wonderful agent, who has stuck by me through thick and thin.